What had she done? She had only wanted time to think, but her harsh decision had ruined her life forever…

"He's not talking to me," Patricia confessed to Naaki a week later when they met for breakfast at Infusions.

They'd just finished an early morning appointment with her dressmaker to resize her maid of honor outfits for the traditional and white wedding ceremonies, since she'd filled out a little due to the pregnancy. Thankfully, she still didn't look pregnant, just curvier, and the dressmaker had even complimented her on her figure. At the compliment, guilt had jolted through her, and her heart had constricted with a stark reminder of the reason for her new curves and the man responsible for it…the man she'd lost forever.

Abandoned by her father at a young age, beauty therapist, Patricia Owusu, has learned the hard way that men can't be relied on. She's determined to make it on her own without falling into the cultural trappings of marriage. However, when she finds herself pregnant after a torrid love affair with African-American financial consultant, Ty Webber, she discovers one man's resolve to stick around.

When Ty discovers Patricia is carrying his baby, he offers marriage, because real men take responsibility for their actions. He isn't prepared for Patricia's stubborn determination to make it on her own. But nothing will prevent him from claiming his child or the woman he considers his.

Can Ty convince Patricia to take a chance on him to help provide a loving home for their baby, or will Patricia's mistrust lead her to miss out on true love and rob her child of the type of father she never had?

KUDOS for *Expecting Ty's Baby*

In *Expecting Ty's Baby* by Empi Baryeh, Patricia Owusu does not believe in marriage, so when she ends up pregnant—by a man who lives an ocean away, no less—she is determined to make it on her own. But when the man she won't admit she has fallen for comes back to Africa for their best friends' wedding, Patricia finds herself even more deeply in love. Still, she refuses to depend on any man, especially one who doesn't even live in her own country. Can he convince her to trust him and give their child two parents, or is she doomed to be unhappy forever? Well written, enchanting, and heart-warming, this is one romance fans should love. ~ *Taylor Jones, The Review Team of Taylor Jones & Regan Murphy*

Expecting Ty's Baby by Empi Baryeh is the second book in her Love from Ghana series. This story takes up where *Chancing Faith* left off, with everyone getting ready for Naaki and Thane's wedding. Naaki's best friend, Patricia, and Thane's best friend, Ty, had a brief week-long affair when Ty was in Africa a few months ago, and now Patricia has discovered that she's pregnant. But when Ty finds out that she is expecting his baby, he is determined to marry her and be a father to the child. Patricia is just as determined to go it on her own, believing men to be undependable since her father abandoned her when she was a child. Can these two stubborn people find some common ground for the sake of their love and their child? Poignant, charming, and full of wonderful characters, *Expecting Ty's Baby* will warm your heart right down to your toes. A wonderful love story and a worthy addition to the series. ~ *Regan Murphy, The Review Team of Taylor Jones & Regan Murphy*

Dear Reader,

Thank you for picking *Expecting Ty's Baby*. This is the second instalment in my From Ghana with Love series. No problem if you haven't read book 1, Chancing Faith. You can enjoy this as a standalone novel, although if you're like me, then you're anal about starting the series from the beginning (no pressure).

Expecting Ty's Baby has one of my favorite romance tropes: secret pregnancy. I love babies, and I enjoy reading books about two people drawn together by the wonderful life they've created.

Ty and Patricia were secondary characters in Chancing Faith who stood out with their fun personalities, and I knew they had a story to tell. Their past relationship allowed me to up the ante on the heat level of this story. Pairing Ty, an African-American, and Patricia, an African, brought out some conflicts that might surprise (and hopefully delight) you.

As many of you demanded, there is even more cultural flavor woven into the fabric of this story.

Expecting Ty's Baby wasn't an easy story to write. Although it had one of my favorite romance themes, I struggled to find a balance between the romance, the sex and the culture, but (if I may say so myself) I believe I finally struck a balance that works.

I hope you enjoy this new trip to Ghana with Ty and his journey of love with my Ghanaian beauty, Patricia.

I love to hear from readers. Please visit me online at: www.empibaryeh.com.

mP

Expecting

Ty's Baby

Empi Baryeh

A Black Opal Books Publication

GENRE: MULTI-CULTURAL ROMANCE/BLACK ROMANCE

EXPECTING TY'S BABY
Copyright © 2019 by Empi Baryeh
Cover Design by Kimberly Killion
All cover art copyright © 2019
All Rights Reserved
Print ISBN: 9781644371077

First Publication: MARCH 2019

Published by Black Opal Books **http://www.blackopalbooks.com**

Expecting

Ty's Baby

Chapter 1

Accra, Ghana:

Patricia Owusu flicked a coin into the air, deftly catching it between her palm and the back of her other hand. "Heads, I tell Ty he's going to be a father; tails, I don't."

Across the table in their usual corner of the Infusions Café where they met for breakfast one Sunday every month, her best friend and blushing bride-to-be, Naaki Tabika, quirked an eyebrow. "Pat, don't even joke about something like this. Ty has a right to know."

"Who says I'm joking?" Patricia lifted her hand to reveal the coin and her heart sank.

"Heads," Naaki said with a smile. "Clearly, fate knows what it's doing."

Patricia waved the pesky coin. "Best two out of three."

Naaki laughed, and despite herself, Patricia gave into a smile. Okay, so maybe she *was* half-joking, because deep down inside—if she let herself think about it, allowed her mind to reach past the pregnancy hormones and the nerves jangling in the pit of her stomach—she couldn't deny the temptation to tell Ty. An idea that sounded good only in theory, because in truth, Ty wouldn't want to know.

"The last thing I want is to noose a lifelong commitment around a guy's neck."

Especially one resulting from a liaison that lasted all of one week. They had both known—*agreed*—their relationship had no future.

Naaki looked doubtful. "I don't know. Ty struck me as a responsible guy, and I'm sure he'd like to be involved in some way."

That was the problem. He hadn't said it in so many words, but Patricia had sensed Ty to be the kind of man who took obligations seriously, so telling him would mean forcing his hand.

"I can't let him take responsibility for something he didn't sign up for. Besides, his life is in America, mine is here. What kind of life would he be offering my child?"

"You know it's no excuse," Naaki said. "Remember when *I* didn't want to get involved with Thane because he would be returning to America? Look at us now."

As Naaki refilled her cup, the diamond solitaire on her engagement ring caught in a ray of sunlight, which had managed to slip through the branches of moringa trees lining the side of the quiet street their table overlooked.

It paled in comparison with the gleam in her eyes.

"I'm happy things worked out between you and Thane, but it's not the same. For one, you two were in love pretty much from the start. Ty and I aren't."

Even though their attraction to each other had been instant, the passion between them seemingly insatiable, there had been no gray areas in their agreement: *one week, no strings attached.*

A baby came with major strings.

Pushing aside those thoughts, she concentrated on her tea as though she'd find some secret solution in the dark brew. "I told him I was safe. I *thought* I was safe; and now to tell him I'm pregnant? He's going to think I'm a liar. Or worse, one of those women who get pregnant to trap guys into marriage."

"Hey." Naaki's hand closed around Patricia's arm. "You're neither a liar nor one of *those* women, and if he spent any amount of time with you, he should know. Besides, you're both consenting adults. It's not as if you forced yourself on him."

"Well..."

Warmth spread through her veins, and her heartbeat quickened as the memories came back in vivid color. They'd been cuddling in the king-sized bed in Ty's hotel suite. After going through their pack of condoms during the night, she'd thought the multiple orgasms he'd drawn out of her had been enough to last a lifetime—or at least a few years—but she'd woken up to his kisses on her shoulder and gentle caresses along her thigh.

He'd nudged her backward, bringing her butt in contact with his hot, throbbing arousal and all previous orgasms were promptly forgotten. She'd wanted him with a fierceness she'd never experienced with any other man. She'd turned, thrust her pelvis against his hardness, and practically assaulted him. Not that he hadn't been a willing participant. *Au contraire.* He'd been—

"Uh, Earth to Pat," Naaki's voice broke through her lustful recollection. "Wow, it's been what? Three months? And you're still spacing out at the mention of his name."

Patricia blew out a breath of pent up frustration then

sipped her tea in favor of wasting any effort in trying to deny the truth of her friend's words. She was no prude, but sex with Ty had been beyond her expectations.

She sighed. He'd been so attuned to her needs, touching her as if he'd known her body for much longer than a week. He'd branded her in a way she wasn't sure could be replicated. Would her body ever get over him?

She shoved the thoughts out of her mind, squaring her shoulders in a false show of indifference. "It doesn't matter. We're never going to see each other again, so what's the point? What he doesn't know won't hurt him."

"Him or you? Don't assume Ty is going to make the same choice your father did."

Despite Naaki's gentle tone, her words delivered a heavy dose of tough love, its sting worse than a back-handed slap. Patricia steeled herself, forced her mind to move past it.

"My parents married because my mother got pregnant with me and look how well that turned out." Sarcasm. An ineffective shield against the torment of unanswered questions simmering beneath the surface, but it helped in a way she couldn't explain. "All I'm saying is men have to be ready for a baby. Otherwise, they run in the other direction."

"Who says Ty isn't ready?"

"Trust me, he isn't," Patricia said with conviction, her mind going back to their conversation one early dawn as they pillow-talked after a night of mind-numbing, limb-weakening sex. How had he put it again? *Not in my ten-year plan.* The words echoed in her head, along with the rich timbre of his laughter as he'd said them.

Absentmindedly, she fiddled with the coin she'd flipped as those thoughts continued their torturous flow. She wasn't an indecisive person by nature, but she had a huge decision to make, and the consequences would be far-reaching, whichever direction she went.

"I still think you should tell him," Naaki said. "I mean, hopefully you wouldn't be showing yet, but as my maid of honor it would be a *little* obvious if you have to excuse yourself every few minutes to go and throw up."

"What are you talking about?" Patricia's mind whisked past the barb, reading between the lines. "You don't mean he's—"

A prickly sensation skittered up her spine—something between dread and excitement—at the thought she didn't want to speak into existence.

"I do," Naaki answered. "Ty is coming to the wedding. He's the best man."

Patricia buried her face in her palms. This complicated things. Big time. It would be easy to keep the truth from him when they lived thousands of miles and an ocean apart. It was an entirely different story to share the same space with him and not blurt it out—a definite possibility if he trained those haunting green eyes of his on her, eyes which tempted her to say things she shouldn't.

Like the morning they'd made the baby now growing inside her—the only time during their weeklong affair they hadn't used a condom. She'd asked him to make love to her, and he'd whispered in his deep baritone, "We're out of condoms."

With disappointment crawling up her stomach, she'd done a quick calculation, determined her period had ended about a week earlier, just before they had met. She'd deduced she was still safe for another couple of days—at least.

Since they'd already had the all-important HIV status talk before they had sex the first time, she'd confidently uttered the four fatal words. "It's okay, I'm safe."

"You know, the best man and maid of honor have to spend a lot of time together," Naaki teased. "If last time was anything to go by, then you won't be able to resist him."

But Patricia had to.

For his own sake.

And hers.

"Like you said, I won't be showing yet," she persisted stubbornly. "I'm sure I'll survive a few weeks without cracking."

ℰℐℰℐ

It took thirty minutes of walking in circles and passing the same neighborhood shop three times before Ty Webber admitted it.

He was lost.

Gazing reflectively at the somewhat familiar surroundings, he took in a row of neem trees overhanging the white walls of a gated property and the roadside mechanic up ahead. He had to be in the right neighborhood. However, many streets around him were unmarked as was typical with non-major roads in the city—something he'd observed on his first visit to Ghana three months ago—and there were just so many landmarks a person could memorize.

Bringing his mind back to his predicament, he contemplated his options, the most logical being to catch a taxi back to his hotel. However, he was eager to see Patricia. It should have worried him just how much he wanted to see her, because it sure as hell wasn't about the things they needed to do as best man and maid of honor of their best friends' wedding.

No. There was just something about Patricia, something which evoked thoughts of her at the most inopportune times. Like a couple of weeks ago during dinner with a very beautiful woman, all he'd been able to think about was how his date approached the food with passionless indifference, as though eating were a mere formality. He'd only been half listening to her, while the other half of his mind had reminisced about dinners with Patricia—how she'd close her eyes and moan whenever she tasted something she particularly liked, how he'd thought they sounded erotic until he'd made love with her, and she'd moaned and whimpered in his ears, and he'd—

Damn. There he went again thinking about her when he needed to make a decision—find her or return. He thought about the best man's to-do list in his jeans pocket: a pretty standard list, and having been best man three times already, he knew the drill. However, this being only his second visit to Ghana, he would need help finding his way around. So, on two counts, he needed Patricia.

Five minutes later, he'd retraced his steps back to the junction where he'd dropped from the communal taxi he'd picked up in front of the hotel. At a few minutes past four o'clock in the afternoon, temperatures were cooler than they'd been a few hours back. The Harmattan season prevailing in early-January had cast the atmosphere in a dry, dusty haze.

Despite the reduced humidity compared to what it had been on his first visit, he'd worked up a light sheen of perspiration from the short walk. However, having escaped from a harsh winter in New York, he wasn't complaining. He found a shade in the shadow cast by a kiosk marked "*Lotto.*"

"Good afternoon," he said to the young man inside.

It was another thing he'd noticed on his last trip. People greeted as they passed each other on the street. The friendliness strangers showed one another had staggered him. Though he'd only had two weeks to spare on his last visit, the experience had been intensely spiritual;

one that had deepened his desire for a greater connection to Africa—his roots. He'd left knowing he'd return.

So, when Thane had called and asked him to be best man at his wedding, Ty hadn't needed any convincing.

"Good afternoon, sir," the young man answered, an eager gleam lighting in his eyes. "You want to stake some lotto?"

Ty chuckled. "Oh no, thank you."

As a financial consultant, his job was to understand how money worked. He spent hours daily, advising clients on where to invest, whether a potential venture would be worthwhile, and a whole array of other financial issues. The outcome of lottery was just too random for him to put any stock in it.

That wasn't to say he didn't believe in luck or chances. Meeting Patricia had been purely accidental. A little over three months ago, he'd been contracted by Black & Black, a US advertising agency, in a merger with one of Ghana's top agencies, Media Image Advertising—or MIA as it was generally called. Having spent two years in Britain obtaining an ACCA, the equivalent of a CPA in the British-based system, he was in a better position than most of his American counterparts to audit accounts on behalf of clients back home.

He'd been in one of a series of discussions with Thane, who at the time had been the International Account Director for Black & Black, on whose recommendation Ty had been hired. The meeting had been interrupted when Thane was called to an emergency conference call with a client. Normally, Ty would have remained in the boardroom and continued working on his own or used the break to check the latest headlines on CNN online. Yet something had drawn him out, beckoned him to get some fresh air.

He'd been just in time to see Patricia walk into the

main reception, an African goddess, her skin a flawless cocoa brown much darker than his caramel complexion. High heels added a couple of inches to her five-seven frame. She'd been wearing skinny jeans and a fashionable blouse made from African print fabric. Slung over one shoulder was a handbag, and in her other hand she held, of all things, a silver toolbox. His curiosity aroused, he'd lingered at the entryway.

She'd flashed an even set of pearly whites at the receptionist and asked for Naaki, whom he'd had the pleasure of teasing his best friend about a few times before. Moments later, when the two friends hugged, Ty had still been watching, unable to will his legs to move him past the spot where he stood. He'd also guessed Naaki would take her visitor to her work area in the general office, which meant they'd have to walk past him. Although, he'd only known her a couple days, he'd sensed Naaki to be too polite to pass by him without introducing her friend, so he'd casually slipped a hand into his pocket and waited.

The sound of a horn blaring yanked him out of his thoughts and he swore, realizing he'd drifted off again. Whipping out his cell phone, he made a mental note to get a local line, since the wedding was six weeks away, and using his US phone for a month and a half would be expensive and even impossible at times.

He dialed Thane's number.

"Hey, buddy," Ty said when the call went through. "You don't happen to be with your bride-to-be, do you?"

Thane's chuckle drifted across the line. "You tried to find her on your own, didn't you?"

Ty grimaced, and gave Thane a moment to have a laugh at his expense.

"What did I tell you?" Thane asked.

Don't go on any bold expeditions. Ty hadn't forgotten. He'd just been so sure he'd make it to his destination without trouble, so he hadn't called to ask Patricia to meet him at the hotel as his friend had advised. He'd wanted to surprise her.

Still, he refused to admit his error—unless he really had to. "Before you think of making me beg, bro, just remember I'm your best man and I could—"

"Wow, even with your hands tied behind your back, you're threatening me." Thane laughed. "But you win. Naaki won't forgive me if I let you do anything to ruin our wedding."

Before Ty could think of an appropriate response, another voice drifted across the line in the background—a female. *Naaki*. He breathed out in relief when he heard a rustling sound suggesting the phone had changed hands.

"Hello, Ty." He could hear the smile in Naaki's voice. "What's this I hear about you ruining the wedding?"

"Just trying to get you on the phone, Naaki," he said with a smile of his own, hoping he sounded apologetic enough.

After a few more pleasantries, he explained his situation to Naaki, and as he listened to her instructions, it became clear where he'd gone wrong. He thanked her and spoke with Thane briefly again before clicking off.

Armed with the new directions, he found himself on the right street within seven minutes. The house, a one-story structure, looked like many of the buildings in the vicinity, the top part being residential with the bottom floor reserved for commercial purposes. In Patricia's case the space below the one-bedroom apartment had been empty, the shop which had previously been there having gone out of business a few months back.

It had been locked up at the time of his last visit, with old newspapers covering its glass front. Today, though the paper remained, some parts no longer sticking to the glass, the door lay open. New owner, he guessed, immediately dismissing it from his mind. He had better things to think about.

He'd almost bypassed the entrance on his way to the side gate that would grant him access to the staircase leading upstairs when a movement in his peripheral vision made him turn. He stopped short at the sight meeting his gaze. Patricia?

His pulse kicked up a notch, and he had to hold in a breath for a few seconds to steady his heart. Ridiculous, he told himself, hesitating for a moment. He didn't do this. He didn't go back, *never* dated any woman twice. His policy had always been to keep his relationships short, sweet, and noncommittal. Once it was over, it was over. Like the first time with Patricia—the rules had been simple and his return to the US put a distance between them, ensuring the permanency of their goodbye.

He continued to watch her tap away at her computer, oblivious to his presence. She sat with her back to him, her long braids held up in a way that displayed her graceful neck. He could hear music, an eighties hit he suspected was streaming from the laptop which claimed her full attention.

He didn't do this, but here he stood, and truth be told, he wouldn't mind spending another week with her.

Or maybe six.

Finally, he crossed the threshold.

"Hello, Trish."

Chapter 2

Patricia froze, her eyes involuntarily closing as the rich timbre of the deep voice bathed her skin in tiny tingles and stole the breath right out of her lungs. There was only one man on earth whose voice could affect her that way.

Ty Webber.

The man who'd managed to put her in a tizzy for over three months, even without being physically present. God only knew what the effect of seeing him again would be. She had no desire to find out, but he was here, and she'd have to face him at some point.

"Trish?"

She let out a slow breath and braced herself for the sight of him as she opened her eyes and swiveled around. For several moments, she just stared. Nothing had changed since she'd last seen him. He was still delicious to the eyes, still devastating to her system. At over six feet, with a body honed to perfection, Ty looked more like an American footballer than an accountant, and his sheer presence threatened to reduce her to hormones and nerve-endings.

Her gaze raked the length of his body before settling on what was exposed of his face. His flat cap left her with only a view of his nose and the finely trimmed beard gracing his strong jaw line.

He reached up and slipped the cap off his head, leaving her unprepared for the impact of his shocking green gaze, then he stepped forward, and the room seemed to shrink around him.

"No, *akwaaba* or *etisen*?" he asked.

The Akan expressions—"welcome" and "how are you"—rolled off his tongue in a deep, sexy rumble with just a hint of his American accent. It sent a shiver slicing up her spine, and she could have sworn something fluttered in her lower abdomen. She stiffened. Surely eleven or twelve weeks was too soon for her baby to kick or respond to outside stimuli no matter how earth-shattering?

He hadn't released her from his gaze when he came to stand in front of her. "How have you been?"

There was that damn flutter again. She had to fight the urge to put a protective hand over her belly. Something she'd caught herself doing often lately, even though she wouldn't be showing for…well, she hoped at least six weeks.

"I'm fine," she answered.

Thankfully, he stepped aside, giving her some much-needed breathing space and leaned against the table counter. He cast a glance around before turning to her again, his look curious.

"What are you doing in here? Last I remember, the landlord had locked up and was looking for a buyer."

Phew. Safe topic.

Patricia breathed easier, raising her hand in a guilty-as-charged gesture. "You're looking at her."

"No kidding." His expression held admiration, and pride swelled in her chest. "When you talked about opening your own beauty shop, I thought you meant in a more distant future."

"Me too," she admitted.

That had been a more pessimistic side of her. The idea to stop working from her proverbial suitcase and start the shop had come to her almost five years ago, and she'd been saving for four years now. She'd even drafted a short business plan, but the statistics of failed business ventures always left her thinking she needed more time, more planning, more money.

"You made me realize I wasn't as unprepared as I thought."

Before Ty, she'd only shared her plans with her best friend, but somehow, he'd managed to get her talking. Perhaps his background in finance had convinced her to open up. He'd appeared impressed by her vision and had asked to see her business plan. After reviewing it, he'd done some quick financial projections and told her, matter-of-factly, she had a good plan.

She found herself smiling in recollection of the rush she'd experienced after talking with him. "You gave me the push I needed."

"You'd make an excellent client, then. If only I could get my sister to take my advice as seriously."

"Sister?" The last time they'd been together, they hadn't talked about family—at least not in anything more than passing statements, and neither had probed. It had been necessary, because getting attached hadn't been part of their agreement. This time, no deal existed, and she couldn't help giving in to her curiosity. "Older or younger?"

As an only child, she often wondered what it would have been like to have siblings. Whether they were complaints laced with affection or childhood pranks, sibling stories held a fascination she couldn't explain. Gazing expectantly at Ty, she wondered if he'd answer the question.

"Older," he provided. "Unfortunately, Gabby seems to have difficulty seeing me as anything other than her kid brother."

A tiny snort of laughter slipped past Patricia's lips as her eyes devoured the denim-clad muscular thighs and the fitted mahogany-colored T-shirt paying homage to the rippling planes of his tight abdomen.

"Has she looked at you lately?"

The words came out before she could stop them, and the resulting heat suffusing her face made her thankful for her dark complexion.

The sound of Ty's laughter left her stunned for several seconds before she realized why. She hadn't heard him laugh before. Not in this hearty, unrestrained manner. If she wasn't mistaken, he even appeared a little...*embarrassed*?

Shyness wasn't a quality she found particularly attractive in men, and she'd never gotten the impression Ty possessed a shy bone. In fact, his self-assuredness had been the first thing that had drawn her to him. Plus, he was gorgeous—he had to be used to receiving open admiration from women, yet her unintended remark had him gazing down at his feet as if, for the moment at least, he couldn't meet her eye. And her heart squeezed into a ball of emotions.

When he looked up, no hint of embarrassment remained. His eyes bore into hers, its intensity thrusting her back to the last time they'd been together—in his hotel room, surrounded by Egyptian cotton, his strong arms enfolding her as they lost themselves in each other.

She gave herself a mental shake, grappling for a safe topic, because she did *not* want her mind to wander in that direction. With the heated look he gave her, she feared where the conversation might lead if she didn't actively guide it away from dangerous territory.

"I thought you weren't supposed to be here for another three weeks," she said, keeping her tone deceptively neutral if not slightly curious. *Perfect.* Now if only she could maintain this momentum until he got back on a plane to America.

"Careful. I might think you're not happy to see me." The corners of his lips curled up, telling her he merely meant it as a joke. "It isn't a busy time of year, so I shifted things around and bought myself an extra three weeks."

"Why would you want three extra weeks here? Don't get me wrong. Ghana is lovely, but I can think of several far more interesting destinations for a vacation."

He didn't seem to share the sentiment, though, because his brows creased into a frown. "Why wouldn't I? I love Ghana, but unfortunately, my last stay was so short I didn't get to experience enough of it, and I intend to rectify that." He shifted, facing her more directly. "Africa's in my blood, woman. I only wish I'd come here earlier."

Patricia chuckled, shaking her head. "You sound like a typical African-American."

"What do you mean?"

"Well, when you people come here—"

"Whoa," he said. "You people?"

Eyes, which a moment ago sparkled with delight, now filled with rigid indignation, staring at her as though seeing her for the first time—and not in a good way. His icy expression locked the rest of Patricia's words in her throat, and she knew she'd crossed a line she hadn't realized existed.

"I didn't mean to—"

"No," he cut in, pushing off the table. "I want to hear what you have to say, Patricia. Enlighten me."

She hesitated. At his full height, he towered over her seated form, looming dangerously like a predator ready to pounce. Her pulse raced. She hadn't set out to offend him, didn't want to have this conversation. She wished he'd just take it as the passing comment it had been, but considering his resolute stare, instinct told her he wouldn't let it rest until she'd finished what she'd started.

How on earth had they gone from practically flirting to…well, this?

"What I meant was…" she began cautiously, searching her mind for words she hoped wouldn't deepen the hole she'd dug for herself. "African-Americans have this romanticized idea about Africa. Coming here seems like a pilgrimage to be made at least once in a lifetime to…I don't know…claim their African-ness or something. But how many of you have bothered to invest any money in Africa? Not many. Because when you take away all the talk, African-Americans don't actually see this as home."

Shit! Out loud, it sounded harsher than it had in her head. She braced herself for a venomous retort. However, as several charged seconds ticked by, he only stared at her, his face drawn in a stiff mask as if he needed to shield himself from her words.

In the silence looming around them, she became aware of every beat of her heart pounding against her ribcage like the rhythm of timpani drums. When he stared into her eyes, whether smiling or in the unrelenting way he did now, it made her want to fill the silence.

Thankfully, he saved her the need to do so. "I see."

Patricia blinked. She didn't know what she'd expected, but she hadn't thought it would be summed up in two words which could mean just about anything. A reminder that though she carried his child, she didn't really know the man.

She did, however, recognize the look in his eyes—

the look of a man whose chord had been struck hard enough to offend. Maybe even hurt. "Ty, I'm—"

"Look," he cut in. "Our best friends are getting married. Maybe we should focus on that. Besides, it's a free world. You're entitled to your opinion." He slipped a hand into his pocket and brought out a piece of paper. "Pre-wedding list from Thane."

It took her a moment to shift gears to the new line of conversation, but she welcomed the change of topic.

"I also made one with Naaki." She opened the document on her laptop. "We can compare notes and formulate a plan for getting everything done." Turning back to him, she added. "It will move faster if we're working together."

"My thoughts exactly."

She stood. "I'll bring you a chair."

"I'll get it," Ty said, stepping forward and—probably unintentionally—closing the space between them.

She stopped dead. Her head snapped up, caught his gaze. Big mistake. Just inches apart, his warm breath fanned her face. Her eyes dropped to his lips, which only three months ago had kissed her and turned her into a whimpering mass of ecstasy. Liquid heat unfurled in her lower abdomen.

His lips parted, and for a second, she thought he might lean in and kiss her.

Instead, he said, "Just show me where to go."

She released a shaky breath, shamed to realize she might have allowed him to kiss her if he'd tried. Swallowing the disappointment she shouldn't be feeling in the first place, she stepped back and pointed to a door behind him. "In there."

As he turned away, she resisted the urge to place her hand over her belly. Nothing said "pregnant" louder than a woman constantly caressing her tummy.

೧౨೪౨೩

Twenty-four hours after their conversation, Ty still bore the sting of Patricia's words. He didn't know why. Intellectually, he realized she hadn't meant to inflict pain, but he'd heard the words and remembered himself as a little kid in school who'd been told he didn't belong in a club he so desperately wanted to join.

The implication of her words—that he didn't belong here—had gutted him like a lance through his chest, segueing into a need to prove her wrong, to force her to see him not as a statistic, an insignificant part of a collective, but as a man apart. Why, though? He had no clue, so he'd bottled it in and zipped his mouth shut. Then spent the rest of the evening resisting the urge to reacquaint himself with her lips.

Stepping through the doors of the restaurant where he was supposed to have dinner with her and the rest of the bridal party, Ty prepared for more of the same. Thankfully, the others' presence should make this a much easier task than yesterday.

A glance at his watch told him he'd made it with only five minutes to spare, which meant he was probably the last to arrive.

He stopped at the reception about to ask after his friends when he saw Patricia across the room. She sat facing the entrance, browsing through what he assumed to be the menu. No Thane or Naaki, he noted.

"May I help you find a table, sir?" the receptionist asked, her customer service smile firmly in place.

"Thank you, but I found my table."

"Very well, sir. Enjoy your dinner."

He mumbled a thank you as his mind fished out an unsolicited memory of Patricia eating. The corners of his lips twitched. He'd definitely enjoy *that*, but the ensuing

R-rated thoughts would guarantee a less than comfortable dinner.

He'd psyched himself for it. Or so he'd thought before Patricia looked up and every resolve he'd built up over the past twenty-four hours vaporized. The impact of her gaze was like having every one of her manicured nails raking down his back. *Lord, have mercy*. He needed to sit before the desire tightening in his groin made a mockery of his resolution to not proposition her.

She laid down the menu. "Hello."

No smile. He'd have bought the arms-length routine she'd been dishing him since yesterday if he didn't sense the sexual undertones in her gaze.

"*Etisen?*" he said.

He may have butchered it a little, for he got a chuckle out of her. "*Bokoo.*"

"Aren't you supposed to say *eyeh*?"

"I could." The right corner of her lips curved up. "But I prefer to say I'm cool."

He took the seat opposite her and promptly realized his error. The chair farthest from her afforded him a full view of her heart-shaped face. Dark brown eyes cast a spell on him, fueled his desire.

"Naaki and Thane are running late," she said. "They asked us to start without them."

Exactly what he'd tried to avoid by arriving in the nick of time, but it looked like fate meant to mess with him.

A waitress showed up and offered him a menu. "Would you like to order drinks?"

He chose a whiskey, she a glass of freshly squeezed orange juice.

After the waitress had left, Patricia said, "I'm sorry I had to cancel this morning. Something came up."

"Nothing serious, I hope."

"Uhm…" She appeared undecided for an instant then shrugged. "It's about the shop. I was advised not to lock up all my savings into setting it up. I read it's better to use only a part of my money and supplement with a loan."

"Makes sense. You want to maintain enough capital to run the business. That's usually a big problem with start-ups."

"At least I'm doing something right." She smiled. "I've been trying to get an appointment with a loan agent at my bank, and they finally called this morning, so I had to drop everything. They're busy people, I guess."

He found himself genuinely interested. "How did it go?"

"Good, I think. He walked me through various options available, gave me some material to read and their application form."

"You don't sound happy."

She sighed. "I don't know. I just expected more, I guess…more care, you know, instead of being treated like a line item in a factory."

The analogy made him chuckle.

"Then again," she continued. "Caring about my business venture is my job, not the bank's, right?"

They were interrupted by the waitress who had come to serve their drinks.

"Are you ready to order now?" she asked.

"Could you give us five more minutes?" Patricia requested, picking up the menu again. "Choosing food can be a long process for some of us."

When they were alone again, Ty raised his glass. "What should we drink to?"

"Beauty by Patricia." The giggle she gave was girlish and infinitely sexy.

He raised an eyebrow.

"The name of my company," she explained, and the sparkle in her eyes just about did him in.

"To Beauty by Patricia," he said.

As their glasses chinked, he almost forgot to think about how much he wanted to get naked with her. Oh, the thought was there, but for the first time since he'd touched down, something else overshadowed it. Pure and undiluted admiration. So sue him, he had a thing for black women who went out there and made things happen for themselves, women who'd refused to allow life to make them victims of circumstance or culture. Patricia was all that and then some, considering she lived in Africa, where the realities facing small businesses were far more dire than those of their counterparts in the US and startups had a higher probability of failure.

"I hope you have a good financial advisor working with you."

She baulked for an instant then nodded. "John Wiley and Sons."

His eyes narrowed. "You're getting financial advice from a *For Dummies* book?"

A sheepish grin later, she answered, "Among others. They have very good information."

"Yes, for someone who needs a quick brush up on a topic, not for someone investing actual money to start a business."

She dropped her gaze, focused on her fingers fiddling with the base of her glass. He reached forward and closed his hand around hers. Electricity sizzled at the contact, and he almost withdrew his hand. Almost.

"You need a professional to guide you through this process."

She tried to pull her hand away. He tightened his grip just enough to stop her. She looked up, and he saw a vulnerability that hadn't been there earlier. Suddenly, what had been a simple desire to see her succeed became personal. The fierceness of it surprised him, frightened him.

"I don't have the kind of money it costs to hire a professional."

"Who said anything about paying? You're sitting in front of one of the best in the world." He gave her a reassuring squeeze. "Let me help you."

She snatched her hand out from under his. Righteous anger flashed in her eyes. "I'm not a charity case, Ty. I don't need your pity offering."

Thunder struck inside him. Her insult melded with the injuries she'd inflicted yesterday, turning his insides molten. He bit down on his tongue, took several seconds to deflect the ferocity lacing the words rushing forward.

Then as restrained as he could muster, he said, "You're full of opinions, aren't you, Trish? Pity offering?" He snorted. "Do you know how much my time is worth? You're the one who spoke of us people not investing here, yet when a legitimate offer comes along, you spurn it. So, what do you really want?"

Every sinew in his body wound tight, he feared they might snap any moment. He hadn't felt this unhinged in decades. Not since he was a kid, angry with the whole world after his father had passed away and his mother decided she couldn't care for her two children. It had taken the unflinching love of his aunt and her family to turn him around, to keep him in school and save him from the many dangers he could have gotten himself into in the hood. Patricia's eyes reflected disbelief, a sheen of moisture had turned them into liquid orbs of onyx. Her lips parted with the beginning of a response.

"Hi, guys." It was Naaki's animated voice, snatching them out of the tension.

"Sorry, for keeping you waiting," Thane said. "I had to meet a few more of my new family."

Ty looked up as Thane pulled out a chair for Naaki.

As she sat, Naaki explained, "Our *Abusua panyin*—" She looked at Ty. "—that's the head of the extended family, wanted to meet Thane and me to discuss the wedding." Turning to Patricia, she added, "Can you believe the family wants us to do a separate *kokobo* before the customary wedding? And then there's the white wedding. Three ceremonies."

"I can't believe you said all of that in one breath." Patricia attempted a laugh and succeeded for the most part, but Ty heard the tremor beneath.

His outburst had upset her, even with his best efforts at reining it in. For that, he was sorry.

"Are you okay?" Naaki asked Patricia. "I hope we haven't kept you hungry."

"I'm fine. Don't worry about it."

Ty looked from Patricia to Naaki. He couldn't help thinking she seemed too concerned for having delayed dinner by little more than fifteen minutes. He turned back to Patricia, his eyes narrowed. Was there something else going on with her?

Chapter 3

Sitting amid animated conversation with jokes being traded across the table, Patricia couldn't muster a genuine laugh. Ty, on the other hand, seemed to be having a good time. Generous with smiles, nothing of his earlier anger showed.

Normally, that would be her. She'd perfected the ability to shove unwanted emotions aside and exist in the moment.

She'd learned the skill following years of spending every afternoon after school sitting on the veranda waiting for her father to return and never having that desire fulfilled.

Her well-practiced talent of faking happiness failed her tonight, relegating her to the sidelines—an outsider looking in. On her right, Naaki and her fiancé, Thane, had slipped into a tête-à-tête on some wedding-related details, while opposite her, the bridesmaid, Shirley, cozied up to Ty, not bothering to be subtle about it.

Whatever she was saying, Patricia doubted it warranted placing a hand on Ty's arm or thrusting her overly exposed double D cups in his face.

Whatever it was, it must have been funny, because Ty laughed, and the sound of it had every feminine part of Patricia thrumming with awakened need. Her fist clenched around her fork.

"Pat, are you all right?" Naaki's brother, Nii, sitting on her left, asked. "You're not talking much."

"Uhm." She shifted in her seat, pried her eyes from Ty and Ms. Breastina. "Yes, I'm fine."

Nii didn't appear convinced, but if he had any inclination to probe, he didn't. Even if he weren't an intuitive guy, surely her rigid posture and inability to summon a simple smile conveyed the message, *I don't want to talk about it*. At least not to anyone sitting at the table. Except Ty.

Like a metal scrap caught in a magnetic field, her eyes went back to Ty. She'd have given anything to not have picked a fight with him earlier. A lump formed in her throat with the realization that he hadn't spoken directly to her since the others arrived a little over an hour ago.

Every time she'd spoken, he'd looked in her direction, but not *at* her. Had anyone else noticed?

"How is your new business plan coming along?" Nii asked. "Naaki says you're finally taking action."

She nodded, relief washing over her at the change in topic. "I have, though it's still at the beginning stages, securing funding especially. I had a meeting with my bank today to talk about loans."

He frowned. "Aren't banks expensive? Have you researched other types of financiers? There are quite a few financial institutions focusing on Small and Medium Scale Enterprises."

"You might also want to explore donor agencies.

Many of them support women entrepreneurs," Thane added.

"Thanks. I'm considering all options."

"If you need legal advice at any point, don't hesitate to ask," Nii said.

"Thanks, I'll keep your offer in mind."

"Don't be surprised if she doesn't, though, Nii," Ty said. "Patricia strikes me as the kind of woman who likes to do it all on her own. Am I wrong?"

He looked at her, his expression hard. She tried to respond, but nothing presented itself.

"Everyone needs help at some point," Nii replied. "No one exists in a silo."

"I completely agree, counsellor." Ty bared his teeth in a smile, belying the sarcasm dripping from each word.

Her heart clenched. No one seemed to pay any attention.

"Hey, Naaki," Ty said suddenly. "This meal is really good. What did you say it was called again?"

Before Naaki could respond, Patricia answered, "*Waakye.*"

Ty turned to her again, and their gazes locked. If she had any sense, she'd look away, because she couldn't mask her desire, and the last thing she needed was for him to know she still wanted him.

"*Waa-chey,*" Ty repeated, though his look didn't soften. Beneath the surface lurked a gleam of hurt, hurt she'd inflicted with her words. Now she understood why he'd avoided her eyes all evening. Regret choked her.

Shirley giggled. "You've *brofo*lized it."

"Okay, what does *brofo*lized mean, aside from the fact that I must have butchered the word despite my best efforts?"

"Wait, I know this one," Thane said. "It's local slang for 'anglicized.'"

"You remembered," Naaki squealed.

"Indeed I did," Thane replied, and they kissed.

Meanwhile, Shirley began coaching Ty on his diction.

I can't do this. Patricia stood. A wave of queasiness swept over her, leaving her slightly off balance. She braced against the table.

Ty stood in a flash. "Trish?"

Oh, when he called her Trish, it always put a kick in her heartbeat, made her remember intimate moments she'd be wise to forget.

She raised her hand, a cautionary gesture meant for him as much as her. "I—I need to use the washroom."

Without waiting for a response, she escaped.

✌✍✌✍

She nearly bumped into someone exiting as she pushed to enter the washroom. Muttering an apology, she stepped aside to let the person pass before entering. Thankfully all four stalls stood ajar signaling the absence of other occupants.

She headed for the sinks. After splashing water on her face, Patricia's agitation seemed to subside. She straightened her posture and took several breaths, which had the desired effect of killing the queasiness. *Thank God.* She had no wish to throw up the delicious mushroom sauce and local brown rice she'd just wolfed down.

Exhaling a deep breath, she stared at her image in the mirror. Physically, she looked fine. Her dark skin, one of her best features, seemed to be glowing. If only she could make her mixed emotions absorb what was displayed on the outside.

The sound of the door opening made her turn.

"Naaki, you shouldn't have followed me in here.

Now everyone's going to think something's wrong."

Despite Patricia's words, concern knotted between Naaki's brows. "Are you sure everything is okay? You haven't been yourself all evening."

"I'm fine."

"Pat, it's me, your best friend. Don't think I didn't notice we interrupted 'something' between you and Ty when we walked in." She made air quotes around the word something.

Patricia sighed. She'd have preferred not to get into this, but Naaki could be persistent. More so now after finding love with Thane. She'd gotten it into her head that everyone deserved to find love.

"There wasn't 'something.' He offered to give me financial advice."

Naaki beamed. "That's wonderful."

"I turned him down."

"You what?"

Patricia grimaced. "Don't look at me like that. Spending too much time with him is a sure-fire way for him to find out about the baby."

"Seriously?" Naaki gripped Patricia's shoulders, and, despite her friend's petite form, it was clear to Patricia that *she* was going to lose this staring contest. "I thought we agreed you were going to tell him."

"It was a coin toss, not a binding contract."

Naaki raised her hand in concession. "Fine, but don't say I didn't warn you when he finds out."

"How is he going to find out if you don't tell him?"

"Well, like my mother always says, pregnancy is like telling lies. The truth will surely come out."

"Hopefully, Ty will be long gone by then."

Just then the door swung open again and Shirley entered.

"Is everything okay?"

"Oh, come on. Can't a girl powder her nose in peace?" Patricia couldn't keep the impatience out of her voice.

Shirley frowned. "It didn't look like you wanted to powder your nose. Besides, didn't you leave your handbag at the table?"

"We'll be there in a minute," Naaki said.

Shirley looked from Naaki to Patricia before nodding.

After she'd left, Patricia turned to Naaki. "Remind me again why she's on the bridal train."

Naaki sighed. "You know why. Did I tell you my aunt called again to thank me? She honestly believes bridesmaids get noticed by potential husbands."

"If you ask me, your cousin doesn't need to be a bridesmaid to get noticed," Patricia responded. "Did you see her in there? She was all *Naa Forfor Nofowaa* in Ty's face."

To emphasize her point, she thrust her chest forward in an exaggerated copy of Shirley's flirtation.

Naaki chuckled. "Well, if she's got it…"

Patricia tossed her friend a look she hoped conveyed her lack of amusement.

"*Konongo kaya.* You don't want him, but don't want anyone else to have him either."

"I *do* want him."

This was the first time in three months she'd admitted it out loud. Before now she'd been bent on denying it, believing if she did it long enough, the feeling would pass.

Before Ty's return, it had been easy living the lie.

"There. I said it. Happy now?" Deflated, she leaned against the sink behind her. "He affects me even more than he did three months ago. I've already broken a couple of rules because of him, so giving in to my desire is just not something I can risk."

"Look, I'm not going to tell you what to do, but you need to figure out what you want quickly, because Ty's here for only a short while. After he goes, it might be too late."

Not willing to draw out the discussion, Patricia nodded. "I hear you. Can I have a moment alone, please?"

"Sure, but don't hide in here too long."

Patricia couldn't help smiling. "I'm not hiding."

Naaki shook her head, giving her an indulgent smile. She held up one hand and said, "Five minutes," before breezing out.

Alone again, Patricia blew air out through her mouth. This overdose of emotions took some getting used to. The hormones from being pregnant shifted her balance but, juxtaposed with the upheaval created by Ty's mere presence, she almost couldn't recognize her life. She needed to figure a way of seizing back control of her emotions or she'd never survive until Ty left Ghana again.

By the time she came out of the ladies' room, she'd made a decision. She needed to call it a night. Usually, she hit the pillows between eleven and midnight, but lately her body's demands had led to increasingly earlier bedtimes. Besides, it had been a long day and a tedious evening, and she wanted out.

As she approached the table, Ty turned and everything decelerated to slow motion, the world around her turning into a blur—all except Ty. God, if this happened *every* time he looked at her, then the next six weeks could be the longest of her life. Their first time together had been short, so most of their time had been spent exploring the pleasures of each other's body and their conversations had constituted of sexy pillow talk.

This time around, they would have so much more

time. If she gave in to her sexual urges, their discussions would surely broaden in scope, pillow talk would graduate in intimacy, which could be dangerous for her heart. Even if she were willing to risk her heart on a relationship with a short shelf life, she had to think about how such an emotional upheaval would affect the development of her baby. She'd have to brave out the maelstrom of desire Ty's presence evoked. *For the greater good.*

When she reached the table, she picked up her purse. "Sorry, guys. I have to go home. It's been a long day, and all I want now is to lie down."

"If you give us a minute to get the check, we can give you a ride?" Thane offered. "Naaki said your car's at the workshop."

"Thanks, but you don't have to cut your evening short on my account. I'll just take a taxi."

"Are you sure?" Naaki's brother asked, checking his wristwatch. "If you still live in Adabraka, it's not a huge diversion for me."

Ty stood. "I'll go with you."

Et tu Ty? She released an exasperated breath. Why were they making a big deal out of it? It was barely nine o'clock, and her neighborhood, while quiet, had the reputation of being one of the safest in the city.

"What kind of best man would I be if I didn't look out for the maid of honor?"

Despite his genial tone, his eyes held uncompromising determination. She took a few seconds to weigh her options then concluded she might be better off giving in. The more she persisted to convince them she was okay, the more curiosity she'd arouse and the longer it would take for her to leave.

Plus, call her masochistic, but among the lot she'd rather go home with Ty.

So much for keeping him at arm's length.

ᏃᎦᎦ

"I don't need taking care of, you know," Patricia said when they stepped outside. Her voice came out low, a whisper, which nonetheless projected in the still warmth of the night.

After several seconds without a response from him, she turned sideways. He stared ahead, his profile stoic. Finally, she heard his deep intake of breath.

He looked at her, and thunder might as well have struck after the flash of...annoyance? Impatience? Incredulity?

"Are you always on the defensive?"

Aggravation. Despite the balmy, breezeless air, Patricia shivered. Perhaps she should have been scared, but she wasn't. Somehow, Ty didn't strike her as the kind of man whose patience wore thin as easily as wind blew away flakes of cotton. Yet, she also realized she'd pushed a button or two between yesterday and today.

She began to say something, but her response staggered as she realized she didn't know how to answer his question. She sighed. "It's always been just me and my mum. I guess I'm simply used to having to stick up for myself."

His look softened. "Trish, I know you're a strong woman. Hell, it's one of the things I admire about you. But did it occur to you I only wanted some alone time with you?"

She couldn't help it. She giggled. "You could have just said so."

"In that case, how about this?"

He faced her fully, subjecting her to a powerful blast of his magnetism. Electricity jolted through her, and she realized he'd touched her; warmth infused her body where his hands bracketed her waist.

The next instant, she was plastered against him, her soft abdomen privy to the state of his desire. His heated breath wafted over her face, a mix of him and the whiskey he'd had at dinner. An avalanche of sensations, fierce and unrelenting hit her in the gut.

Then the worst thing happened. The most embarrassing moment of her life.

She threw up.

On him.

For several seconds, she could only stare in horror at her dinner, now a less than palatable concoction splattered on Ty's clothes and shoes.

He still held her as she doubled over, one hand on her shoulder, the other rubbing her back.

"Trish, what's going on?" He pushed back a few strands of her braids hanging loose from the confines of her up do.

"I am so sorry," she said.

"We need to get you to a hospital."

Crap! Her stomach lurched again, and she figured out what had triggered the emesis. Thankfully, what came out the second time was minimal. She took in a deep breath, exhaling through her mouth. It seemed to help.

Ty held up the bottle of water he'd taken with him from dinner. "Here—"

"Please stop talking," she gasped, turning away from him. "I need a minute."

"This could be food poisoning. You need a doctor."

"I don't, and it's not food poisoning. It's the alcohol."

"You didn't drink."

"No, but *you* did."

His features assumed a frown, his confusion absolute. "You're sick because I drank?"

"I'm not sick. I'm—"

She stopped abruptly, tossing different possible explanations in her head, all of them partial truths. No matter what anyone said, keeping quiet and outright lying were not the same. She wasn't prepared to do the latter, but she'd spoilt her chances of doing the former.

"I'm...uh."

His eyes narrowed. "You're what?"

"I'm..."

Shiiit.

She couldn't believe she was going to tell him. "I'm pregnant, Ty."

Chapter 4

For the next couple of hours Ty functioned on autopilot, focusing on actions and results. Performing a makeshift cleanup. Finding a cab. Getting Patricia safely home. Getting cleaned up—separately. Ensuring Patricia ate again…and most of all, not panicking.

All the while, two words echoed in his ears. *I'm pregnant.* One image engraved on his mind. Of her face deluged with emotions, of the reluctance in her delivery, the apology in her eyes. He hadn't needed to ask. She'd confirmed it, anyway. With words he'd filed away for later scrutiny. *Sorry…never meant for it to happen…don't expect anything from you…*

He'd nonetheless filtered out the unspoken. The baby was his.

For several seconds, he'd stared at her, struggling to get past the disconnection between his legs and the part of his brain controlling his movements, until the honking of a newly arrived cab had snapped him into motion.

The ride back to Patricia's had passed in a blur. Having understood the alcohol on his breath had triggered her nausea, he'd given her as much distance as the back of the saloon car allowed.

On arrival, she'd attempted to get him to leave with the taxi giving the rationale that getting another in the quiet neighborhood may not be possible at a later hour. Despite the logic of her reasoning, he didn't want her to be alone tonight. However, sensing she might be resistant to that notion, he'd proffered the equally reasonable argument of needing to get his clothes and shoes better cleaned. He could have waited until he returned to his hotel room, but he'd hoped to guilt her into letting him stay. It had worked. With shoulders slumped in resignation, she'd invited him up.

Inside, she led him straight to the bathroom, holding the door open for him.

"I keep spare towels in the cabinet." She pointed to a closed inset cabinet behind him. "You can use one after you wash down. Unfortunately, I don't have any clothes you can wear, but I should have a bathrobe you can use until your clothes get dry."

"Thanks."

As she left, he slipped off his T-shirt, but as he unbuckled his belt he had second thoughts. Perhaps he needed to wait for the bathrobe, because although Patricia had seen him naked before, they hadn't discussed the nature of their current relationship.

He took in his surroundings, a cozy space with a shower stall, a toilet and sink, and just enough room to move in between. The soft scent of lavender permeated the air from a potpourri on the window sill.

Gentle footsteps announced her return. At the door, she stopped. He didn't miss the hungry look in her eyes as her gaze lingered on his bare chest then roved down his abdomen. He tried not to let it get to his head. There were more important things going on than his desire to fulfil her passions. He cleared his throat, snapping her back to attention.

"Uhm. Here you go."

Ty eyed the peach-colored silk robe with large red hibiscus flowers.

"It's the only one I have that's big enough."

As he took it, their hands touched, and electricity zapped them. She withdrew her hand and mumbled something unintelligible before turning and leaving.

After a quick shower, he swished some mouthwash in his mouth, and wore his boxers and the robe before putting on a pair of slippers Patricia had left at the door.

He now stood in the kitchen of her apartment, whipping together a quick meal out of some vegetables and chicken strips he'd found in her fridge.

He became aware of the sound of the shower running and the implication—Patricia in there, naked. He didn't want to dwell on it, didn't want to imagine the water on her skin gliding down in adoration of her nudity, or the tiny pools it would form in the graceful dips of her body. A futile endeavor. He became hard in an instant, and the boxers offered no resistance to his growing erection.

He shifted his focus to work, making a mental checklist of financial hurdles he wanted to guide Patricia through as she worked on setting up her shop. Thankfully, by the time he turned off the stove, the tent in the robe had gone down. Keeping his mind on work-related thoughts kept his libido under a measure of control.

It didn't take him long to locate the plates, drinking glasses, and cutlery. For a small kitchen, it amazed him how uncluttered it looked. Just like the bathroom, Patricia had made ample use of the walls to create storage space. No doubt a testament to her organizational skills, which would come in handy after she moved from working from her brief case, or beauty tool box as the case was, to owning a shop and employing additional hands.

As he dished out the food, he noted the shower had stopped running and started bracing himself for the sight of her. He filled a tumbler with juice and set the table. He sat down and waited.

His mind drifted back to the moment when, for several seconds, the world had stopped turning. The initial shock had abated, but a part of him waited in expectation of waking up, while the other part of him didn't want to wake up and discover tonight had been a dream. *I'm Certifiable.*

Awareness slithered up his spine and he knew she'd walked back in. He turned, and everything in him stilled. Even though the wrap dress she'd worn at dinner had been dangerously sexy, she looked more beautiful in an oversized white T-shirt over black leggings and her face devoid of makeup.

The leggings he supposed had been worn for his benefit as he suspected she'd otherwise have gone for only the T-shirt. Or maybe nothing at all?

He cleared his throat and forced his mind to shift focus to the pillow and bedding in her hands.

"Don't worry," she said. "I sprayed the room earlier on, so you'll be safe from mosquitoes."

Ty chuckled. At least one of them had his wellbeing in mind. His gaze followed the alluring sway of her hips as she crossed the room to the living area and dropped the stuff on the sleeper couch she'd offered him for the night. She turned to face him with eyes looking a little sad, maybe anxious.

He struggled to find something to say, something that wouldn't come off sounding like he only wanted to take her to bed. How did he convince her he just wanted to hold her while she slept, whisper in her ear he was here for her and their child? How did he do that while keeping his libido in check?

"Something smells nice," she said, reeling him back.

He managed a smile. "Hopefully, you'll approve of the taste as well."

"I'm sure I will." She smiled, and although the room was illuminated by two ceiling globe lights, it appeared to brighten further. "You said you were a good cook."

"Wow, you remember that."

"I remember a lot."

No four words had ever meant more. The way she'd said them told him their time together had been memorable for her as well.

"Me too."

She joined him at the table, engulfing him in the soft lavender aroma of her bath gel. Contrary to its supposed tranquilizing effect, the fragrance sent blood rushing down to fuel the rigidness of his hard on.

"I'd have been happy with tea or cereal, but I'm definitely going to enjoy this more." She leaned forward and took a long sniff.

He only smiled, certain any attempt to push a response past his suddenly gravelly throat would make him sound like a boy whose voice had just begun to break. She scooped a moderate portion of food into her mouth, and he watched as she sat back and closed her eyes with a moan. A little smiled teased her lips and all rational thinking began to ooze out of Ty's mind. The only thing stopping him from pulling her onto his lap and devouring those luscious lips was the knowledge that far more was happening between them than his desire to take her to bed.

"This is good," she said, looking at him as if she hadn't just guaranteed he'd be nursing blue balls by morning. "Thanks for going through the trouble."

"My pleasure."

Her appetite didn't seem to have suffered, he noted, and finally, the tension which had seized him the moment she'd hurled her dinner on him began to dissipate.

"I love the way you eat," he found himself saying.

She looked at him, brows furrowing. "How do I eat?"

Amusement tugged at his lips as her dark brown eyes bore into his. He said the first thing that came to his mind. "Like you're having sex."

She gasped. "What?"

"It's extremely sexy."

"Do you think about sex every time I eat?"

Despite her shocked response, he could see the light of intrigue lighting up in her eyes. "Let's just say memories of you moaning while eating have tormented me the past three months."

She bit her lower lip, drawing his gaze. He wanted to lean forward and tease the lip out from between her teeth with kisses guaranteed to get her hot and bothered, begging for more.

"I haven't been able to keep you out of my mind either."

"Where do we go from here?" he asked.

Her shoulders slumped, and she shook her head. "We agreed to a clean break."

"A little too late for that, don't you think?"

She nodded.

Several seconds elapsed. He took her hand.

"When were you going to tell me about the baby?"

He met her gaze and she dropped hers, appearing unduly fascinated with the food. Suspicion stole through him—something dark and barely restrained.

His eyes narrowed. "Were you going to tell me about the baby?"

"I didn't think we'd meet again."

"That doesn't answer my question."

She shook her head.

"Are you planning on keeping it?"

Her head snapped up, indignation burning in her eyes. "Of course."

"Then why would you keep this to yourself?"

She blinked rapidly as if staving off tears. Instead of a proper answer, she said, "I'm really sorry, Ty."

"You've apologized many times tonight. What exactly are you sorry about? The baby? Throwing up on me? Or not telling me I was going to be a father?"

"I wanted to protect you."

"Since when is it your job to protect me?"

"I told you I was safe. I didn't want you thinking I manipulated you."

He took her hand again, tried to hold her gaze. "We both made a choice that night, so I'm as much to blame."

"Don't you see? This is exactly what I tried to avoid," she said. "If you didn't know, then your conscience would be clear."

Frustration mounted.

"Oh, you decided to keep me in the dark for my own good? How noble of you." He gave a humorless laugh. "Let me ask you this. What did you plan on telling our kid about his father? That I'd died or abandoned you? Do you have any idea what that does to a kid?"

She looked stricken. "I—I hadn't thought that far," she mumbled. "But this is something you never planned for, and I couldn't, in good conscience, hang it around your neck."

"No. You don't get to decide that," he snapped.

She recoiled at his harsh tone. He pushed away from the table, stood, took several steps away from her in his attempt to reign in the raging emotions, because they weren't aimed at her. They were aimed at the first woman who'd uttered similar words. His mother, the woman who'd chosen her music career over her children. After his dad died, his mother hadn't wanted the responsibility of raising two children on her own, because she *hadn't signed up for it*. Instead of getting a regular job, and taking care of her children, she'd walked.

Patricia hadn't shirked responsibility, though. She'd taken it on, and for whatever reason, she wanted to do it alone. Her next words gave him an idea why.

"What happens when you return to America, huh?" Her lips trembled, her voice barely audible. "What do I tell our child then? What do you propose I tell him or her about why daddy doesn't come around or live with us like other kids' fathers?" Her eyes misted. "I didn't want to tell you, because a few weeks off your busy schedule every year isn't going to be enough, and I can't watch my child's heart break a little each day you aren't here."

A sob sounded from her, and she turned away before he could see her tears fall. He'd never been at ease around a crying woman, but somehow Patricia's tears only roused his protectiveness. He wanted to wrap her in his arms and promise her everything would be okay. Closing the distance between them, he placed a hand of comfort on her shoulder.

She shrugged it off and sprang to her feet, though she didn't move away. He pushed aside the chair standing between them and stepped closer. Lavender invaded his senses again, surrounded him, this time accompanied by her own unique scent.

"Turn around, Trish. Look at me."

She sniffed, muttered a muffled, "No."

"I'm sorry for yelling at you."

She didn't answer. His need for a physical connection became too intense. He couldn't wait any longer.

Surrendering to it, he wrapped his arms around her.

"Don't—" She cried, trying to pull out of his arms.

"Shh." He hugged her tighter. "You don't have to do this alone."

He didn't keep track of the number of times he whispered assurances in her ear, but eventually, she abandoned her efforts at breaking free and collapsed in tears. He continued to hold her as the sobs shook her body, each one reaching into him, wrenching from him feelings he hadn't believed existed within him.

Gradually, the tears subsided, and he got her to turn around. The air whooshed out of him with one look into her emotion-darkened eyes. As he stared into their liquid depths, his mind registered the way her curves melded against his body. She fitted in his arms like she belonged there. He didn't want to let her go.

Not yet.

Not ever.

"You don't have to do this alone," he repeated, needing to see belief and acceptance in her eyes.

She shook her head. "I'm so used to relying on myself. I don't know how else to do it."

"I do."

She palmed his chest, sending shockwaves rippling through him. He shuddered at the impact, groaned when she pressed into him, her softness against his hardness, her body demanding his attention. He tried to take a mental step back, having promised himself tonight would be an innocent one, no matter how much he wanted to touch her. That was before she turned her brown eyes on him, showed him the passion burning in their depths, and he knew his personal promises were all but broken.

"Honey, let me stand by your side."

She stared at him for a long moment until electricity began to crackle between them. He wanted her so much now, he ached, but he made no move to satisfy his need.

"Kiss me," she whispered.

His labored breath matched hers. With every exhalation, the space between them shrank. He should say something. Stop her. Because, surely the discovery of impending fatherhood required homage in the form of self-discipline. But her lips were so close...just a breath away. Her heartbeat vibrated into him, firing his pulse, overriding restraint.

"Trish..."

Their lips touched. Passion flared. *Holy*...

Time shifted, melding the past with the present until it disappeared altogether. With a tilt of her head, she slid her tongue into his mouth, reminding him of its velvety exquisiteness. She damn near stopped his heart. Neither memory nor wishful thinking over the past three months had come close. This was perfection. Having her in his arms, feeling her, tasting her again. She filled his senses, inebriated him with her essence. In a frenzied motion, he tipped her backwards. Her gasp gave him better access to her mouth and he suckled—lapped—feasted...

Chapter 5

O *h. My. God!*
Every cell in Patricia's body screamed with utter joy. If she hadn't stopped thinking the moment she'd turned and stared into his eyes, she might have been worried about the ferocity of her heartbeat. However, Ty's tongue ministering to her mouth, his hands singeing her through her T-shirt, his hard length searing her abdomen, made her oblivious to anything other than him.

The ground shifted under her feet, causing her to gasp. Slicing her eyes open, she realized Ty was raising her onto the sideboard a few feet from the dining table. She hadn't noticed when they'd crossed the distance between the two.

Ty pulled back slightly, and his Adam's apple bobbed. "Damn."

A giddy sensation galloped up her spine.

"I had every intention of not touching you tonight," he said. "Or at least, discussing first whether we wanted to do this."

"It's a little unfair to ask after you've already kissed me." Her voice came out husky. He had to know how much she wanted him. "If you're asking, the answer is yes, I want this."

"Good," he said in a voice equally thick with desire. "Then it's time to show you what I wanted to do the moment you walked in here wearing your oversized T-shirt."

He slipped his hands underneath her T-shirt, lifting it. She raised her arms to allow him to take it off, but as the garment got halfway over her face, he left it covering her eyes and raised arms.

"Uhm, what are—"

"Shh."

Before she could think or speak again, his mouth closed around her nipple. She moaned her pleasure. She tried to remove the T-shirt, itching to touch him, too, and realized only then that he'd knotted it over her arms. She gasped, although she wasn't sure whether it was due to the imprisonment of her arms or the pleasure he meted on her nipple.

"Hold still," he commanded softly as his hand slipped between her parted thighs.

Sucking one nipple through her bra and stroking her crotch, Ty had her whimpering in no time.

"I want to touch you," she pleaded.

"You'll get your chance."

The teasing in his voice, the hunger, conspired to stoke up her passion. He stopped his caress long enough to slip his hand past the waistline of her tights. She parted her thighs a little more, rocked her pelvis forward in anticipation. She sucked in a breath as his fingertips fondled her pubic hair. Thankfully, he didn't linger there too long. He swept aside the seat of her panties, found her swollen bud, which had breached the confines of her labia. A cry of pleasure ripped out of her.

"You like that?"

She nodded then realized maybe he couldn't see her face.

"Yes," she moaned.

"Say it."

A rush of delectable sensations exploded in her. She loved when he made her admit her need, her passion. Only *he* could make her surrender to his possession, his pleasure.

"I like the way you touch me."

The last word came out with an "oh" as he flicked her nipple with his tongue. She writhed, rocking her hips faster. Her inability to touch him tortured her, but it also focused her mind fully on the pleasure he doled out. Every one of her sensory nerves had become supercharged and transmitted a unified message to her brain cells. *Ecstasy.*

"Say it again," Ty whispered.

All she could offer was a moan, echoing of intense pleasure, as she moved her hips in rhythm with the strokes of his finger.

"Say it, Trish."

She floated, the sounds of her enjoyment flowing softly from her lips.

"I like—the way—you—" She gasped as the onset of her release rushed at her. "Oh, Ty—"

Her release swept her with the force of a tidal wave. She rode it to its highest peak, crying out, then whimpering as it brought her back to shore.

Ty eased the T-shirt off her head, allowing her to pull out her arms. In the same breath, he swooped down, cradling the back of her head in both arms and kissed her deeply. His erection pressed at the apex of her thighs, extracting residual spasms in her inner walls.

Patricia pulled back, energized by her satiation. She

looked down at the evidence of his virility. With a tug, the belt unraveled, and the robe fell open. He shrugged it off, letting it fall in a heap at his feet, exposing him to her view. *Haaaaah.*

She swallowed, took in his sheer maleness. Her tongue sneaked out to lick her dry lips. "I want to taste you."

"You'll get your chance," Ty said, though there was no mistaking the delight in his voice, the satisfaction of knowing how he affected her.

"If you put those lovely lips of yours on me, I'm going to come in your mouth." He cupped her feminine mound, letting the tip of his middle finger press into her opening. "And I want to come in here."

Patricia sucked in a breath at the impact of his touch, the promise in his voice. She wanted him *now*.

Ty leaned in, stopping just breaths from her lips, "What do you say?"

She didn't need to be asked twice. Grabbing the waist of her tights and panties together, she pushed them down her hips, angling her body to slide them off each butt cheek in turn—a task, which became exponentially difficult when Ty started to kiss her, and impossible after he slipped his hand between her thighs, found her slick heat, and entered her with two fingers.

Her pleasured cry disappeared in his mouth, but that didn't diminish the echo of her aching need. She moved her hips in rhythm with his fingers. Her hands had abandoned the effort of getting her naked, leaving the tights around her knees. One hand curled around him, frantic fingers skidding over his back muscles, while the other hand encircled his engorged member. She squeezed him, explored his length and girth. God, he was glorious— smooth and hard and throbbing.

He pulled back suddenly, leaving her momentarily

disoriented, until he reached for her tights and panties, pulled them all the way down her legs. Her brain cells shifted into gear, and she kicked the garment off. Finally, as naked as he, she proffered her invitation with parted thighs. He stepped toward her, girded his hand around her waist, and pulled her forward until she was settled around his crown.

She held her breath, as he prodded her entrance, shuddered when he penetrated her with his tip. He pulled back.

She whimpered.

He moved again, going just a little farther before pulling back again.

"Don't tease me, Ty."

He grunted, filling her to the hilt in one lunge, and Patricia nearly wept for joy. How had she survived without this for three whole months?

For several seconds, neither moved, except for breathing.

"I remember this," Ty whispered.

"I could never forget," Patricia moaned.

She held him tight as he pulled back and then filled her again and again and again. She welcomed each invasion, cried out his name each time, her only consciousness being of the knowledge that only Ty could ever turn her insides into a volcano about to erupt. Only Ty could satisfy her desire.

"Only you," she gasped.

As if he knew exactly what she meant, he answered, "Only you, Trish."

She closed her eyes, took everything he gave. "Don't stop."

"Never."

"Oh—Ty."

Her climax started deep inside where his body hit the

end of her inner wall, detonated, leaving nothing untouched. She held on tight, maintaining the rhythm as each thrust squeezed out a new wave of release. As her inner sheath contracted around him, he shuddered with his own climax.

Then he went completely still and for a long moment, they simply held each other until their breathing had slowed down to normal. Finally, he loosened his arms and pulled back.

He shook his head. "You're incredible."

Patricia swallowed. Still reeling, she was all emotion and little else, and his words set off a whorl of sensations she had no experience handling.

"Let me be here for you." He placed a hand on her belly. "Both of you."

Whether it was what he said or how he said it, her heart swelled to breaking point and her attempt at a response only made her lips quiver. If he kept this up, she risked falling for him. Instead of treating it like the trap it was and taking a mental step back, her mind decided to dwell on the moment.

Tomorrow she'd worry about everything else— dealing with the aftermath of telling Ty about the baby, of having sex with him, of changing her mind about him sleeping on the couch.

"Would you hold me tonight?"

He nodded, leaning in and kissing her lightly on the lips. She wrapped her arms around his neck.

He began to move her from the sideboard. "Hold on tighter."

She did and locked her legs around his waist, buried her face in the crook of his neck and closed her eyes while he took her to the bedroom.

❧❧❧

Ty lay awake for a long time after Patricia had fallen asleep. He'd never been the kind of guy who took pleasure in watching a woman sleep, but for the life of him he couldn't think of anything he'd rather be doing than listening to the rhythmic sound of Patricia's gentle breathing. As he stroked her arms, she snuggled closer, releasing a contented sigh, a smile tugged at the corners of his lips. When they made love, she was passionate, ravenous—a tigress, but after, when she was replete, she slept like a baby.

His mind drifted back to the last time he'd had her in his arms like this—the night he'd broken all the rules.

He shifted his attention back to Patricia's sleeping form, his gaze drifting down and settling on the rise and fall of her stomach.

Pregnant.

He'd gotten used to the idea and found himself...well, expectant. He'd always known he'd settle down some day, have kids, do the whole white picket fence thing. Growing up in a neighborhood where single moms and absentee dads were commonplace, he'd always be grateful for the loving environment his aunt had fostered in her house. With five kids of her own in addition to Ty and his sister, there had been a lot of mouths to feed and not a lot of money to do it with. All of which had cemented his resolve to be responsible if he ever became a dad.

He'd vowed to never fall into the trap of having children before he was able to provide financially for such a responsibility. When he became monetarily stable, he realized he only wanted to have children with the right woman, but with a thriving career that placed major demands on his time, he wasn't in a hurry. He'd always been careful not to lead on any woman and make her think they had a future when they didn't.

When he wasn't seeing anyone, he saw nothing wrong with having a holiday affair, which is what his time with Patricia was to have been. Their attraction to each other had been intoxicating, but they'd both recognized it for what it was, what it could only be—a short, no strings attached liaison. She'd even insisted on never sleeping over.

Ty had known then that he'd met a female who wouldn't misconstrue what they had.

As their last day together drew to an end, however, he'd found himself wishing for a little more time. That night, after Patricia had drifted off to sleep after hours of lovemaking, he'd been tempted to turn off her phone and keep her from waking up early enough to go back to her place. He'd managed to talk himself out of it, but it seemed fate had nonetheless favored him, because her alarm had failed to go off.

For the first time in his adult life, he'd gone against his time-tested rule of always using protection, because against reason, he'd felt safe with her. Funny enough, his only regret—no, his only *worry* was how the results of his actions affected Patricia. Starting a new business and having a baby at the same time wouldn't be easy.

Sighing, he rolled onto his back, gazing up at the ceiling and listening to the droning chirps of crickets outside. Such a contrast to the night sounds in New York or his old neighborhood in Nashville, Tennessee, where he'd grown up. While musing about that and other disparities between his life in New York and his current frame of mind, he drifted off to sleep.

When he woke up again, the sun poured in its mid-morning brightness through the open louvered windows. It took a moment for his eyes to adjust to the light, and once they did, he turned sideways to the other half of the bed. Empty.

He could hear her, though, and the aroma wafting to his nostrils made his stomach growl with approval.

"I'd still have preferred her in bed," he muttered to his stomach.

He took in a lungful of the crisp morning air before getting up. At the foot of the bed was a trunk on which lay a wrap. Since his clothes were probably still on the bathroom door where they'd hung them to dry last night, he took the wrap from the trunk and secured it around his waist. He surveyed himself in a full-length mirror hanging behind the door. Orange was definitely not his color.

He exited the room, crossed the short corridor separating the bedroom and bath from the living area. Just as he entered the living area, Patricia emerged from the kitchenette with two mugs in hand. She paused, her gaze sweeping down his bare chest and settling somewhere in his midsection, and desire flared in her eyes.

He moved his hips hula style. "See something you like?"

She laughed, continuing her way to the dining table. "Maybe I should have left you the pink one instead."

"Ha, funny."

She placed the mugs beside two covered plates. "I hope you're hungry."

"Very."

"Great. Follow me."

He caught her by the waist and pulled her into his arms in the manner of a man at ease with himself and his woman. As the desire in her eyes intensified, so did his.

"You didn't give me a chance to kiss you good morning."

He lowered his head and placed a soft kiss on her lips...and then another...and another. Then he captured her lower lip, suckling it gently until, with a moan, she invited him into her delectable mouth.

He was just warming up when she broke the kiss.

"The food is getting cold."

"I'm not hungry anymore," he whispered.

"Well, *I* have to eat." She poked a finger at his chest. "And *you* have to replenish your energies."

"Yes, ma'am."

His stomach chose that inopportune moment to growl, forcing him to concede and release her from his hold. They both looked down at the bulge in his wrap.

She patted it as she sat. "Down boy."

That, of course, had the opposite effect.

"If you play with fire…"

He let the sentence hang, mostly because he knew if he continued talking about his desire and what he wanted to do with it, he might be tempted to disregard their need for food. And he really was starving.

He watched her pour already brewed tea into the mugs from a flask on the table. She then uncovered the plates to reveal scrambled eggs and a veggie stir-fry on one, and on the other, medium-sized fried cakes she called buff loafs.

"Dig in," she said.

He picked one. It was soft and warm, and because he hadn't seen a microwave in her kitchen, he asked, "Did you just make these?"

She nodded.

"How long have you been up?"

She only laughed, and the sound of it surrounded him, filled him with a lightness of being he'd only ever experienced with her. She squeezed honey into her tea.

"Naaki got me into the habit of substituting honey for sugar," she explained. "Her father has a bee farm."

She offered him some, but he preferred his breakfast beverages black with no sugar, so he declined. Instead, he bit into the buff loaf. It was good. He began to comment on it, but as usual he got caught up in her first reaction to the food.

She looked at him and gave a sheepish grin. "Sorry. I'm really hungry."

He shook his head but didn't otherwise respond. Her gaze locked on his, and she paused.

"What?"

"You're beautiful."

She gave him the kind of smile people wrote poems and love songs about. "Thanks."

She bit on her lower lip. He didn't know if it was an unsuccessful attempt at holding in the smile, but it looked cute as hell. Neither of them spoke for a stretch.

As Patricia polished off her breakfast, Ty continued to watch her, remembering to sip his tea a few times. He had three words on his mind, three words that had occurred to him sometime in the night while he lay awake. Now, they'd seized a hold of him, demanding to be heard.

Eventually, he voiced them.

"Let's get married."

"What?" The fork dropped from her fingers, falling with a clang onto the plate. Her eyes widened, her lips parted again then shut without a sound.

The pin-drop silence expanded around them, but Ty could almost see the wheels of her mind turning, raising all the reasons why she should turn him down. He knew he had to say something before she gave voice to any of them, so he used the most obvious of arguments.

"Come on, Trish. Our child needs both a mother and father, and I plan to be there for both of you."

Her lips parted, but before anything came out the sound of ringing pierced the air, causing her to start. She checked her phone and then looked back at him.

"It's my mum. I have to take it."

Chapter 6

Patricia stood, putting some distance between herself and Ty. Still reeling from his surprise proposal, her hands trembled slightly as she hit the answer button.

"Maame," she said in the calmest voice she could muster.

"Baaba Patricia," her mother bellowed across the line.

Patricia's spirits sank. Trouble followed whenever her mother used her day and given names together. Hopefully, she wasn't calling to complain about her medication, which she hated taking because she didn't trust doctors or western medicine. For someone with a heart problem, her mother could be stubborn. Three months ago, when her mother had suffered a lapse, due to skipping her medication in favor of trying some new traditional concoction she'd heard about, Patricia had had to spend some time with her mother in Cape Coast, and it had been a daily struggle getting her to take her medication.

"Maame, is everything okay?"

"Why haven't you told me there's a new man in your life?"

Patricia's heart lurched. She jerked her head, span round to check if the main door to her apartment was still shut—bolted, in fact.

Resident two hundred kilometers away, in Cape Coast, her mother wouldn't travel to Accra without informing Patricia, but the conviction in her mother's voice and the actual accusation sent a stream of panic through Patricia's veins. When her mother didn't walk through the door, the tension in her shoulders and neck relented, but only just.

Ty was by her side in seconds. "You okay?"

She covered the mouthpiece of her phone as best she could.

"Shush!" she said, before realizing he'd mouthed the words.

"Hello? Are you talking to someone? Is he there with you?"

"No!" she insisted, although she feared it might be a fruitless effort. At nearly fifty, her mother's hearing acuity was still very much intact. Whatever her mother thought, Patricia needed to nip it in the bud right now. "*Oyeh* TV *no.*"

She avoided Ty's gaze, hoping he hadn't figured out she'd called him the television. She moved away from him again, as if her mother might see him through the phone. Already Patricia wondered if her mother hadn't developed some superhuman abilities.

What were the odds of her asking about Patricia's "new boyfriend" on the morning after Ty had spent the night? Had she spoken with Naaki in the past couple of days, and had her best friend somehow mentioned Ty? It was all the rope her mother needed to resume her campaign to see her only child married. Patricia really *really* didn't need that right now.

"Anyway," her mother's voice drew her attention back to the phone. "I've been talking to Menaesi and she said—"

Patricia bit back a curse. *Menaesi,* her mother's aunt and a self-proclaimed soothsayer. A combination of outrage and relief flooded her. Even though her mother swore by Menaesi's "prophesies," Patricia had never put any stock in what she could only classify as an eccentric woman's ramblings. After all, the woman had predicted Patricia's father would regret his actions, which didn't come true or he would have returned to them.

"Maame, Menaesi doesn't know anything about me or my life. You really should stop encouraging her."

Usually, Patricia would laugh off stories of her great aunt's predictions. Yes, some of them did come to pass, but with her aunt at over eighty years of age, Patricia figured the old woman had seen enough in life to make educated guesses about various things. It didn't make her clairvoyant.

Her mother sighed. "So, no boyfriend then?"

"No, Mum."

There wouldn't be one anytime soon either. Ty would leave in a few weeks' time, and after him, no man's touch could make her come undone the way he did. Besides, she'd soon be a mother, and having herself been raised by a single mum, she knew most men didn't want to raise someone else's child.

"You know I only want what's best for you," her mother said.

"I know, Mum, but there isn't a formula to it."

"Your father used to say that."

Silence followed her mother's words. Maame rarely mentioned her husband, but whenever she did Patricia could still hear the sadness, the disappointment.

"He loved you," her mother continued. "You know that, right?"

Tears stung Patricia's eyes. "Yes."

Knowing that made it hurt the more. If her own father, whom she actually believed loved her, could abandon her, then what chance did she have with other men?

As if she'd read her mind, her mother said, "Not every man will disappoint you, Baaba."

Patricia didn't want to have this conversation, especially not in Ty's presence. She shot a glance around and realized he'd left the room. Still, she decided to switch the conversation to Fante and hopefully end it before he returned.

"How can you still feel that way?"

"I may not have been lucky in marriage, but I have enough friends with good men." She sighed. "The truth is, after your father, I don't think I put much effort into finding another man. I was too brokenhearted to love anyone else the way a wife should. It just wouldn't have been fair."

Her phone beeped, causing Patricia to check her wall clock. "Sorry, Maame, I have to go. We're meeting Naaki and Thane this morning to finalize the seating plan for the reception."

"Okay. Say hello to Naaki for me."

"I will."

"Think about what I said. Don't use me and your father as an excuse to reject a good man."

"Let me guess, Menaesi's advice."

"No, my daughter. This one's from me."

Despite herself, Patricia laughed. "I hear you."

She said goodbye and hung up. Letting out a sigh, she sat back closing her eyes. The sound of footsteps made her open her eyes again. Ty had returned. He now stood in front of her, his eyes mirroring concern.

"That sounded like a heavy conversation," he said.

"It was."

He sat by her, making her skin tingle at his nearness. She refused to let that cloud her judgment, especially after those three words they were yet to discuss.

"Ty, I'm sorry if last night somehow gave you the wrong impression—"

"Wow," he interrupted. "So this is what *that* feels like."

"We can't get married."

"You like me, don't you?"

"Like?" She had to laugh. "Even love isn't a guarantee of a lifetime together."

"We're having a baby, Trish."

"That doesn't mean we should get married."

"It means that while many people get by okay with only one parent, sometimes none at all, every child should have two parents. Ideally, married."

Patricia recoiled from him. Her disdain at his words was so overpowering, she could almost taste it and puke on it. "Ty, please don't go caveman on me right now. Using a baby as an excuse to marry is the worst thing we can do for our child. Believe me, I know this first hand." She stood. "I'm sorry, but I can't marry you."

She glanced at the clock again. They were going to be late for their meeting with Naaki and Thane.

Ty's gaze followed hers as he stood. "We need to get going, but this conversation is not over."

He started to walk toward the door leading to the bedroom. Seeing no other option, she followed him. Just as they entered the corridor, he stopped abruptly and turned. She had no time to react and found herself plastered against him. He cupped her face, and before she realized what was going on, his lips were on hers. Any words of protest died away as her whole being went ablaze with desire.

This was crazy. She shouldn't be reacting this way after the conversation they'd just had. Her rational mind knew this, but her body had taken control. Her lips parted at the prodding of his tongue, her mouth welcomed him, and her body melted against his. She was seconds away from wrapping her arms around him and surrendering, when he broke the kiss.

She swallowed, stared as the gentle breeze of his breath fanned her face.

"I intend to marry you, Patricia," he whispered against her lips.

His words hung between them for several charged seconds before he released her and walked away, leaving her staring at the bathroom door he'd just shut.

ഗ്രൗ

With adrenalin running amok in his veins, Ty paced the breadth of the small bathroom, which was no more than four steps to and fro.

"Caveman," he muttered.

He had no idea why the word grated him, but after mulling over the events of the last half hour, he conceded she had every right to call him that. After all, the only reason he'd offered was for the baby, and then he'd proceeded to kiss her as if asserting some sort of ownership. Instead of telling her the truth—that he wanted to marry her not only because they were having a child together but because, ridiculous as it sounded, he had feelings for her.

It had hit him during the night, while lying there staring at the ceiling and reliving what should have been a simple hook-up. He'd finally acknowledged what had been at the back of his mind all this time: the reason he'd wanted that one last night with Patricia three months ago—why, despite having only known her a week—he'd felt some kinship with her, why he hadn't been able to get her out of his mind, and why the thought of seeing her again had found him mentally rearranging his schedule so he could spend more time in Ghana.

He stopped pacing, stared at his reflection in the mirror.

"So why didn't you tell her, buddy?"

He gave a snort. She wouldn't have believed him. If he were in her shoes, he wouldn't believe him either.

"You knew she'd say no, didn't you?"

Still, he'd gone ahead and proposed. *Idiot.*

He sighed, shedding the wrap. Maybe he'd asked because he sensed his feelings weren't one-sided. But Patricia was stubborn and complicated, and it would take a lot of work to convince her to open up to him, to admit he had a special place in her heart. Like he'd told her, he wasn't giving up. Not until he knew for sure it wasn't her pride talking and that she truly cared nothing for him.

సౠ

Patricia had been dying to talk to her best friend from the instant she'd gone against her better judgment and invited Ty into her apartment. She and Ty had met their best friends and the wedding planner at the glitzy Movenpick Ambassador Hotel, the venue of the wedding reception, and she'd had to endure two hours of discussions on décor and who should sit next to whom.

Eventually, after the wedding planner had left, and Ty had gone with Thane to fit their suits, Patricia and Naaki decided to grab lunch. Luckily, the hotel had a buffet setting, so they didn't have to waste time ordering and waiting for their food. After choosing a table, they ordered drinks before heading to the buffet. While surveying the selection, she couldn't hold it in any longer.

"Ty stayed over last night."

Naaki grinned as though she'd expected that.

"Aw, shut up," Patricia said, which earned an even bigger grin from Naaki.

"Did you two…you know?"

"Is sex the only thing you think about these days?" Patricia rolled her eyes. "Yes, we ended up in bed together."

Naaki chuckled as she went for the salad. "And?" She looked at Patricia. "Come on, you're usually more forthcoming with details."

Patricia hesitated before blurting out, "This morning he asked me to marry him."

"Ooh, that good, huh?"

"Look, this is serious."

Naaki's smile faded and she frowned. "Really?"

"Exactly! Thank you. Crazy, right?"

Patricia hadn't stopped thinking about Ty's words before he'd stormed into the bathroom. *I intend to marry you, Patricia.* Like a threat, and the resolve in his eyes should have scared her. Maybe it did a little, but it also upped her curiosity, even left her a teeny bit…excited.

She swore. *Crazy, twisted, stupid…urgh!*

"I didn't know he felt that way."

"He doesn't. He's a Neanderthal who wants to marry me because I'm carrying his child."

"Okay. Back up. You told him about the baby? What happened to the coin toss?"

She shrugged. "I lost, remember? Besides, I had to tell him after I hurled on him."

"Hold it right there. This is definitely not a conversation I want to have on the go. We need to sit." As she poured some Italian dressing on her salad, Naaki added, "Are you done?"

"Just a sec."

In her eagerness to talk, Patricia had been following her friend without serving herself. Now, she surveyed the options and decided on the spicy garden egg soup. She dished out a portion and grabbed a bread roll. Luckily, the drinks arrived just as they took their seats. No one would interrupt them.

Patricia related last night's events after she and Ty had left the restaurant. By the time she ended, Naaki had on a Cheshire cat smile.

"This is like a period romance," she teased. *"Lady Patricia and the Rake."*

"Stop it," Patricia said, but Naaki continued as though Patricia hadn't interrupted.

"Ty has the perfect physique too: big and tall. He could just pick you up and whisk you off into his chambers."

"Would you focus and help me decide on a plan?"

Naaki giggled, and despite the sense of urgency closing in on Patricia, she found herself shaking her head and giggling too.

"This isn't funny, you know. I need a way to make him understand marriage is a bad idea."

Her friend raised her ringed finger. "Helloo."

"I mean for me and Ty."

"You already told him no, right? So, what's the problem?"

"And I quote." She lowered her voice to mimic Ty's baritone. "'This conversation isn't over.'"

Naaki became serious. "Isn't there a part of you that's a little bit interested in a long-term relationship with Ty? The way I see it, you wouldn't be agonizing over it if you weren't interested."

Patricia considered it a moment. "I admit, I'm curious."

"Plus, the sex is good."

"You're such a romantic." Patricia shook her head. "Good sex does not make a marriage."

"You're not eating."

Patricia looked from Naaki's almost empty plate to her nearly full bowl. With a sigh, she picked up the bowl and brought it to her mouth, taking a long sip of the soup until she'd downed half of its content. Probably not the classiest thing to do at a five-star hotel restaurant, but the pit in her stomach needed to be addressed faster than a soup spoon could do.

She exhaled through her mouth. "So good."

"Now that you have some food in you, and you aren't freaking out, let's think rationally," Naaki said. "I'm not saying marry him right now, but you like him, and you're interested in the possibility of something more. You're about to have his baby, and he wants to do the right thing."

"The right thing is taking responsibility for the baby. Marrying his baby mama is just crazy."

"Why?"

"Because you don't just walk away from marriage."

Naaki frowned. "Are you afraid he's going to walk away or that you are?"

"What?" Only then did Patricia realize what she'd said. She buried her face in her palms. "Oh God. I'm turning into my father."

"No, you're not. You've just never met a man who's affected you the way Ty does, and maybe it scares you."

Naaki's observation made sense, but it didn't improve Patricia's disposition. If anything, it compounded her confusion. She'd always been careful about relationships, not getting emotionally involved. Even with Ty, even when she'd first realized being with him felt different, even after the pregnancy test came back positive—she'd been bent on using her head instead of her heart. Now her feelings were all tangled up, and she didn't know what to do.

$$\mathscr{Chapter}\ 7$$

When Patricia woke up two days later, her mood matched the sunlight streaming in from her windows. Sunny and clear. For one, she hadn't seen or spoken to Ty for a couple of days. Yesterday, she'd spent most of her morning on a home visit with one of her longest-standing clients for a manicure, pedicure, facial, and full body massage. Working had taken her mind off Ty and helped her focus.

With no wedding-related activities scheduled for today, chances were she'd be able to work on Beauty by Patricia without any interruptions. She decided to spend her morning reviewing brochures from five top banks in Ghana she was considering getting a loan from to supplement her savings. Without additional funds, she wouldn't be able to get all the salon equipment she needed in order to cash in on the upsurge in demand prior to the Easter holidays. The other option of using her savings would lock up a significant portion of her capital and leave little cashflow to run the business.

After breakfast she got her laptop and went downstairs to the shop where she preferred working. Even though it was minimally furnished, being in there reminded her of how far she'd come with her dream. Besides, working in here brought a sense of accomplishment, assured her she'd truly taken a step closer to setting up shop.

Once she'd settled down, she checked her emails. As she'd hoped, she'd received a few applications from an ad she'd placed in the papers for salon staff. Only five so far, but she was excited that anyone had expressed interest in her yet-to-be established shop. Well…not to brag or anything, but she wasn't a newbie in the business and her name was somewhat recognizable.

Plus, her celebrity clients had given her permission to use their names in her promotions. Some had even started tweeting about Beauty by Patricia, and some had hundreds of thousands of followers.

She downloaded the résumés but didn't review them in favor of waiting until she received a few more. Besides, the more important task for the day was to assess the public documents and decide which bank to get a loan from. After spending an hour carefully reading through each of the brochures, she went online to check out the published annual reports. She hadn't expected it to be an easy task but after a couple of hours, she found herself drowning in numbers, percentages, and financial jargon.

She sat back, rubbing her neck. This would take longer than she'd hoped. Maybe she should have taken Ty up on his offer of financial advice. Her phone rang, providing a welcome break. She didn't recognize the number.

"Hello?"

"Hi."

Ty?

She'd half dreaded, half expected an unannounced visit from him. Even though she hadn't done as much work as planned, she would have done less if he'd shown up. His presence would have messed with her concentration, but this phone call was a nice surprise.

"Hi," she said.

"How are you?"

"Fine." She smiled, leaning on her elbows so she could continue massaging her neck with her free hand. "I've been working."

"Me too."

She frowned. "Really?"

"Yeah, Thane needed me to vet some books for MIA."

"Oh?"

MIA was one of the top advertising agencies in the country, but it had a special place in Patricia's heart for an entirely different reason. It was where her best friend had met the love of her life. Thane had been in the country to negotiate a merger between MIA and his then employer, Black & Black, but things hadn't gone as planned. MIA had been in financial strain, and when Black & Black pulled out, Thane had taken over majority shares of the company and moved his whole life to Ghana just to be with Naaki. MIA was also where she'd met Ty.

"Hello? You're quiet." Ty's voice reeled her back. "Are you okay?"

"Yes," she said. "Do you know this is the longest phone conversation we've had?"

Previously, their phone calls had been to arrange where to meet.

At the sound of his laughter, something unfamiliar expanded within her, and she had to hold her breath to mask the spike in her pulse in case it manifested in her voice.

"Ty?"

"Hmm?"

"If your offer to give me financial advice still stands, I'd like to take you up on it."

A stretch of silence followed. She checked the screen briefly to make sure the call hadn't disconnected. It appeared to still be on.

"Hello?"

"I'm here."

"Listen, if you've changed your mind, I understand."

"When do you want to start?"

She exhaled her relief. "Tomorrow?"

"I'll be there in the morning."

They said their goodbyes, and she disconnected the call. Having sorted that out, a new spurt of energy bubbled inside. Instead of the break she'd been contemplating, she decided to catch up on news. Returning to her laptop, she opened new tabs in her browser and clicked on her bookmarked news sites.

As she browsed the headlines, the side bar caught her attention. It was a call for proposals for a grant called the African Women Entrepreneurs Development Fund— AWEDF, for short. She clicked on it, praying it wouldn't turn out to be a fake advert or the newest malware on the market.

The page, when it loaded, appeared to be legitimate, providing more information about the program, which aimed to support women entrepreneurs of African descent. Excitement bubbled through her as she devoured the information. Noting the submission deadline was only a week away, she made a list of all the information and documentation she'd need.

When she finally logged off her laptop nearly forty minutes later, she thought she'd burst from the overflow of elation. Between opportunities like this and Ty coming over tomorrow, her optimism about the future of Beauty by Patricia refused to be suppressed.

ೞഔೞ

Ty stared at the phone for a few seconds after he clicked off, his mood pensive. Did that just happen? To say Patricia's turnaround was unexpected would be an understatement. He'd still been contemplating whether to let her suffer the consequences of her decision or launch a plan to change her mind. His surprise and delight didn't come from her asking but how she'd asked. He couldn't put his finger on it, but something about Patricia today felt different in a way he really liked.

He wanted to see her. His every instinct urged him toward giving Thane an excuse and rushing to Patricia's side, but when he stood, it wasn't to pack up and hurry to her place. He covered the short distance to the window of the upstairs office where he had been working since nine o'clock. His gaze flickered absently over the busy Ring Road East dual carriageway, his mind focused on Patricia.

How she'd managed to sneak past his defenses, he had no idea. The physical attraction was there, sure, but he'd also seen a bit of himself in her. Twin souls? He supposed it stemmed from them both growing up without a father.

He smiled, remembering his dad. Ty had only been nine when Ty Webber Senior had suffered a fatal stroke, but twenty-four years hadn't dimmed Ty's memories, and he knew exactly what his dad would say. *A real man takes responsibility for his actions*.

"I'm trying, Dad," he muttered.

A knock on his door brought his attention back. He turned just as Thane entered.

"I came in earlier, but you were on the phone."

"Yeah," Ty replied. "Patricia called."

"Things getting serious between you two?"

Ty frowned then realized why the question sounded odd. Thane probably didn't know about the baby. If he did, he'd know how serious things already were. "You could say that."

Thane paused, his brows raised questioningly. "Really? That wasn't what I expected to hear."

Ty knew what was coming. After all, just a couple of months earlier, he hadn't passed up the chance to tease Thane about his feelings for Naaki.

As expected, when Thane spoke again, he did an impression of an anchorman. "Breaking news. The elusive Ty Webber may have been snagged."

Ty shook his head and gave a snort of laughter. "Man, that's just juvenile."

Thane sniggered. "Seriously, I hope it works out. Patricia is a lovely woman."

"Yeah, she is," Ty said.

He considered telling Thane about the baby. No doubt Naaki knew, but considering Patricia had wanted to withhold the news from even Ty, maybe he ought to wait. Besides, he'd prefer to share the news when he knew where he stood with Patricia.

He expected more teasing, but instead, Thane grew serious as he came to stand next to Ty.

"Remember what you told me?" Thane asked. "You said, 'Ask yourself if she's worth a change in your big plan.'"

"And you didn't kick some sense into me?"

They both laughed.

"Listen, I came to find out if you wanted to take a break," Thane said. "I have a meeting in downtown Accra. Thought you might like to tag along."

"Hell, yeah."

Ty took advantage of every opportunity for seeing as much of Accra as he could, immersing himself into the heart of the homeland. He'd been told about the traffic and the chaos in the central business district, but he'd also heard of the open market, the art center, and a host of other attractions. Hopefully, while experiencing the sights, he might forget how much he wanted to see Patricia.

Yeah, right.

ⱰⱰⱰ

The next morning, Patricia was ready at eight thirty. Though they hadn't agreed on a time, she was certain "morning" meant before ten o'clock, and she didn't want to risk not being ready when he arrived. For one, she'd have to invite him upstairs to wait while she finished getting dressed. If three nights ago had been any indication, being alone in her apartment with Ty was asking for trouble. Being alone with Ty—*period*—could land her in a whole lot of delicious problems. Although considering how their last time together ended, maybe she needn't worry so much.

In any case, her excitement at the prospects for Beauty by Patricia rivaled temptation. With Ty reviewing her financials, she could be confident of making the right decisions and making them quickly enough to meet her target opening date.

She'd brought down all her documents and an extra chair for Ty. Since she had time to spare, she checked her emails and started completing the grant application then performed some searches on new trends in beauty therapy and salon management. She'd been at it for thirty minutes when the knock she had been anticipating sounded. Even though she'd been expecting him, she still found herself holding her breath at the sight of his massive frame silhouetted against the sunny early morning sky.

His smile was easy, happy. "Hi."

She released her breath slowly, her eyes devouring him as he approached. *Stop staring.*

He stopped in front of her. "I hope I haven't kept you waiting."

"Not at all."

She offered him a seat, which he lifted with one hand and turned around so he could straddle it. Why on earth did she find that so alluring? He'd just picked up a chair for crying out loud, but the way his muscles had bunched up with the effort was so...*masculine.*

He turned to her. "You look nice."

Okay, so she'd worn a flirty dress, with a halter neck and an empire cut that screamed *female*, and every feminine cell in her body tingled at the appreciation in his eyes. It only lasted a moment before he became all business.

"Tell me about Beauty by Patricia and how it differs from what you do now."

"That's easy. Right now, I work from a proverbial suitcase—a sort of concierge beauty therapist," she explained. "I do consultancies on makeup and skin care, as well as massage therapy. The bulk of my business comes from occasions—weddings, awards, pageants, and so on, but I have a few retainer clients I see monthly. It's usually by appointment, but Beauty by Patricia is supposed to add to it."

Basking in his rapt attention, she explained her vision of expanding her consultancy services, setting up a beauty academy for training, and eventually starting a product line for dark-complexioned African women like herself. "This shop will also increase my customer base by catering to walk-ins, and potential clients who may need to book appointments when I'm working." By way of clarification, she added, "I switch my phone to voicemail when working, but having the shop means people can call here and book appointments, which would reduce the number of potential new clients I'd lose simply because they called, and I couldn't answer."

Ty nodded, looking thoughtful. "That's quite a list."

"But doable, right?"

"If you pace yourself and are realistic about your expectations, I don't see why not."

Pride swelled inside her, making her realize how much she'd needed to hear those words from someone other than her mum, and it didn't get better than an international finance consultant of Ty's caliber.

He quizzed her further, taking notes, appearing satisfied with most of her answers, and asking her to elaborate on certain points. More than that, some of the questions highlighted issues she hadn't considered at all. After forty minutes of the Q&A, he finally relented and turned his attention to the bank loan documents.

Patricia sat back watching him. He looked so engrossed, you'd have thought he was doing it for himself or getting paid. After she'd rudely spurned his offer the first time, it surprised her he'd said yes so easily. She'd expected to beg and cajole, before getting another chance. She was used to people showing kindness in exchange for something, particularly when the person in need happened to be female, a single woman at that.

In fact, the decision to work for herself had been a result of having to turn down one too many job offers, because someone expected sexual favors in return for employing her. She wasn't used to benevolence. What did Ty have to gain from doing this for her? Could she accept his kindness as a selfless act?

"Why are you helping me?"

He looked sideways at her then sat up straight, turning his chair so he could face her directly. "Because you're everything I think Black women should be." After a moment, he added, "And more."

His gaze locked on her, as his words echoed with meaning.

"I—I don't know how to respond to that."

"It's a good thing you don't have to then, isn't it?" Without another word, he returned his attention to the financial statements. "The good news is a couple of these appear to have good prospects, but these two." He shoved aside the two in question. "You definitely don't want what they're offering."

She was still processing the significance of what he'd said, the ultimate compliment. *You're everything.* Could Ty be for real?

"Look at this." He pointed at something in one brochure, reeling her back. "Annual fees and commissions. You want to avoid that. Besides, if you study their annual financial statements there are too many red flags." He shook his head. "You might want to look at other options. I've done a bit of research of my own and discovered some non-bank lenders you may want to consider. I picked out a few and studied their statements for five years running."

"You did research on this?"

She'd probably missed the whole point of his speech, but she couldn't help it. Her brain cells were yet to kick back into gear.

"I take any job very seriously."

"If I'd known, I wouldn't have asked to meet today. I'd have given you more time."

He raised his brows. "You think I did all this last night?"

"I only asked you yesterday."

He now smiled. "Let's just say I knew you'd change your mind."

"Oh?"

So arrogant. Yet so sweet.

They continued working for a little more time until Patricia couldn't absorb any more information. She stood, stretching.

"You're tired," Ty said. "Let's continue tomorrow."

"Oh, I can't," she said. "I'm travelling to Cape Coast."

"What's happening in Cape Coast?"

"My mother has a doctor's appointment, and if I'm not there to force her, she's going to find a reason to skip it." Seeing his questioning look, she explained. "She mistrusts hospitals, doctors, and Western medicine."

"You look worried." Concern knitted in his brows. "Is it something serious?"

Patricia sighed, contemplating how much to reveal. His eyes stared at her, open and kind, and she found herself opening up.

"She has a heart condition. Atrial fibrillation. It causes an irregular heart rate. She doesn't have a very serious case of it, and if she eats healthy, keeps her stress levels down, and takes her medication, she'll be fine." She let out a breath. "But she keeps going off her medication whenever she hears of some new traditional cure."

Understanding dawned in his eyes. "I see. Are you driving?"

She shook her head. "I wouldn't trust my car even if it weren't at the mechanics. I'm going by bus."

"I'm going with you."

Taken aback, Patricia said, "Er…no, you're not."

"It isn't a good idea for you to travel alone in your condition."

"You're joking, right?"

"Especially not by public transportation."

"In my condition? You do realize pregnancy doesn't make me an invalid."

He pushed himself off the chair, reached for her hand, and tugged her toward him. She resisted, so he moved in, wrapping his arms around her waist. *Seduction won't get you anywhere, mister.* But clearly it would, because she hadn't yet found her voice to protest. Not even when he took complete advantage and kissed her.

When he pulled away, he whispered, "Even Wonder Woman occasionally needs some taking care of." His hands caressed her back. It was distracting, and the gentle persuasiveness in his tone didn't help. "I'll rent a car and we can go in style and comfort. We can set off anytime you say."

She wavered, tempted. "It's not a good idea."

"Because?"

"You can't meet my mum."

"What?"

"She's—"

Her mother had been planning her daughter's wedding since Patricia turned eighteen. Showing up with a man like Ty who looked at her as if he wanted to eat her up would be a big mistake. Luckily, he hadn't mentioned anything more about getting married, but her mum could put the idea right back into his head.

"She won't like you," she said.

"Why not?" He sounded worried.

"You got her little girl pregnant."

"Oh."

The look of disappointment in his eyes filled her with guilt, but she decided not to dwell on it. He seemed to have bought her explanation, which was what mattered.

"Okay, I won't meet your mother," he said. "I'll stay at a hotel, and you can take her to the hospital. There's just one catch. Over the weekend, you can be my tour guide."

She raised a brow. "Isn't it enough you're gate-crashing my trip?"

Her voice had lost all conviction.

He grinned. "What do you say?"

Say no.

"Okay," she said, hoping she didn't regret this decision later.

Chapter 8

W elcome to Cape Coast," Patricia announced, even though they were still in the outskirts of town. They were flanked on both sides by vegetation, punctuated by the occasional building. "Or would you rather I said, *akwaaba*?"

Ty chuckled. "*Me daase.*"

With a sigh, she sat back. "I'm so happy I'm not driving."

"I'm glad to hear it." He glanced at her. "Can we agree that Patricia isn't always right?"

She laughed. "I wouldn't go that far."

To her, Ty tagging along still had "bad idea" written all over it, and when he'd arrived at her place this morning, she'd made one more attempt at getting him to change his mind about coming with her. She hadn't expected to succeed, but she'd seen no harm in trying. She quickly found out Ty had another agenda, which she should have guessed. Cape Coast housed some World Heritage Sites, and Ty had a whole itinerary for his visit—the fish markets, Kakum National Park, Cape Coast and Elmina slave castles, and more.

One look at his eager face as he'd shown her the sheet, and she'd had to relent. In any case, traveling with company often trumped traveling alone, and she'd thoroughly enjoyed the last two hours of easy banter and laughter. Once they reached their destination, however, she planned to drop him off a few houses before her mother's house, just to ensure her mother didn't discover Patricia had come to town with someone of the male variety.

Looking out the window of the rental Nissan Altima, she watched the city slowly unfold before them. No matter how many times she made this journey, it never got old.

"You know what's strange?" she said. "I always find myself de-stressing whenever I enter Cape Coast. There's just something about this town."

"It's clearly more laidback, so it isn't strange to find yourself slowing down."

In another seventeen minutes they were surrounded by buildings, shops, and activity—not quite bustling, but animated enough to not be boring.

"Take a right at the intersection," Patricia instructed. "Almost there."

He did as she directed. They were now off the highway. Patricia found herself impressed with Ty's reflexes as he maneuvered the car around a commercial minibus which had stopped to pick up passengers without signaling. And Ty didn't even swear.

"Sorry," she said. "*Trotro* operators drive to their own rules. You just have to keep a wide berth if you're behind them."

"Don't worry. If you've driven in New York City, you can drive anywhere in the world."

Since she'd never been to New York, she couldn't argue. After another ten minutes, they turned off the main road to an untarred street, and Ty slowed down.

"We'll take the second left turn and then you can drop me."

Ty took the turn and five seconds later, everything changed. Her mother was on the road, walking toward them. Panic unfurled in her, quickly spreading.

Shit! Patricia ducked.

"Uh, Trish? What's going on?"

"Don't slow down!"

"Seriously, what's happening?"

First of all, the car was gleaming new, and with the Accra license plates they stuck out like a sore thumb. Even though her mother walked with one of her good friends, probably seeing her off to the junction after a visit, they were on Patricia' side, and there was no way her observant—*read: inquisitive*—mother would miss her.

"See those women approaching?" she said. "One of them is my mum."

"The one on the left," Ty said. "I see a resemblance."

"Focus."

He'd practically stopped the car, and she could hear her mother's voice getting louder.

This is so not ideal.

"Trish, you do know—"

"Don't say my name," she said between clenched teeth.

"Do you think crouching like that is safe for the baby?"

"Yes," she said, but it was a lie. "I don't know."

According to the pregnancy App on her phone, which gave her weekly updates, the baby was the size of a lime. It was probably fine in there, but the first trimester tended to be the riskiest, so she shouldn't take chances.

Just like that, things shifted into perspective. Keeping her baby safe ranked number one.

Patricia sat up, ready to face the disaster about to happen. They had nearly bypassed each other when her gaze collided with Aunty Dora's, her mother's friend.

She had been in the process of waving down a taxi honking behind, probably trying to tell them to move along, when recognition spilled into her eyes.

"Ah, isn't that Baaba?"

"Baaba?" Her mother turned. "Where?"

"We've been made," Ty said, and Patricia wanted to punch him.

"Baaba." Her mother beamed. "I didn't expect you this early."

Patricia forced a smile, trying not to cringe as her mother inclined her posture to peek inside the car.

"You didn't say you were coming with a friend."

Patricia shot a look at Ty, hoping he saw exactly what she intended. *This is your fault!*

Turning back to her mother and Aunty Dora, she said, "Maame, this is Ty. He's the best man at Naaki's wedding."

"Oh, Baaba. Why are you introducing him on the street as if he's a criminal?" her mother said. "Take him to the house. Let me, at least, give him some water to drink."

In other words, any opportunity to salvage the situation was completely lost. *Great. Just great.*

∽∾∽

Ty hadn't thought Patricia's mum would be the mother from hell, but neither had he expected her to be this hospitable. After they had parked the car and entered the house, Patricia offered him a seat and excused herself saying something about her great-aunt who lived with her mother. She returned just as her mother entered the house.

"Oh, Baaba. Haven't you given your gentleman friend water to drink yet?"

"I went to greet Menaesi." Patricia smiled sweetly at him, but her eyes shot daggers. Had he done something wrong? "Would you like it cold or room temperature?"

"Cold would be great, thanks."

She disappeared around a corner. Ty returned his gaze to the woman sitting adjacent to him, smiling at him with a sparkle in her eyes, eyes which looked so much like Patricia's. Beyond the smile, however, her pleasant oval face bore little resemblance with her daughter's round one, despite his earlier observation.

"I'm sorry if you found me rude outside," she said. "When we receive guests, we don't make introductions on the street. It's considered improper and that's just not the Ghanaian way."

"Ma'am, don't worry. You weren't rude at all."

"You're very kind to say that. You see, before cars were invented, our people walked long distances, so when you received a visitor, the first thing you did was to offer water to replenish them, and as a sign of welcome. These days, it is still customary to offer water to a visitor before you even find out why they are here."

Ty nodded. "Ah."

He loved how such seemingly trivial things had meaning, history, how little gestures like that existed at all. The communal way of living was something he could certainly get used to. Having been rejected by his mother at a young age, he'd grown up learning to be self-reliant, but in spite of it or may be *because* of it, he'd always nursed a yearning for somewhere to belong, someone to choose him. Something many people took for granted.

Patricia returned with two small bottles of water on a small tray. She offered him one, and he noticed she curt-sied as he took it. She served the second to her mother in the same manner. As a guy who found strong-willed and assertive women attractive, he shouldn't find this submissive gesture appealing, but God, it was such a turn-on. He found himself considering different ways he could reward her for bestowing such honor on him.

He cleared his throat, pulling his mind out of the gutter. Those were *not* thoughts he wanted to have in front of her mother, even if mind-reading wasn't a human ability. He took a long sip of the water, the coolness of it hitting him like a dive in fresh springs. Thankfully, it also helped bring his focus fully back to the present.

Patricia's mother came to shake his hand.

"*Akwaaba*," she said. Turning to her daughter who had taken a seat near Ty, she also shook her hand. "*Akwaaba*."

"*Ya'ena,*" Patricia said.

When she returned to her seat, her mother said to Patricia, "Now you can introduce your friend."

"Maame, this is Ty Webber, a good friend of Naaki's fiancé's. He's also the best man at the wedding." Turning to him, she added, "Ty, meet my mum, Ama Benti-Enchill. Most people call her Aunty Ama."

She went on to tell her mother stuff the older woman should already be aware of—why she'd come to Cape Coast. If Ty hadn't already been told about this elaborate custom of introductions and stating one's business, he would have been a little confused. He searched his mental archives for the saying that had cracked him up. *The elders say even when we know your mission, we must ask.*

He snapped back in time to catch Aunty Ama say, "*Yoo. Me ma mo akwaaba.*" Turning to him, she said, "You are welcome again."

Just because he sensed she'd be tickled silly, he answered, "*Me daase.*"

She beamed at him, her kind eyes brightening like Christmas lights. You'd have thought her kid had just said *mama* for the very first time. When she looked at Patricia, he could see the love radiating from her. His chest tightened from an ache that had lain dormant in his heart for a long time, the ache of never having had someone look at him as if he were the best thing in the world. Aunty Ama was a *mom*, not just a mother.

Now he knew he didn't want her to dislike him for any reason.

"I hope you're enjoying Ghana so far," she said.

"Yes, ma'am. You've got nice people, interesting customs, and great weather." Maybe a tad humid, but he wasn't complaining.

"You must try to see some of the tourist attractions while you're here."

"Absolutely."

He had a feeling he'd love Cape Coast from the moment they'd arrived in the outskirts. He'd immediately picked up on contrasts between here and Accra. Where the capital was bustling with commerce and overflowing its boundaries, Cape Coast seemed contained, having a quaintness he found strangely agreeable. After Patricia had mentioned the relaxing effect the city had on her, he'd known Cape Coast would present the perfect setting for proposing again.

Patricia, who had been quiet thus far, now joined the conversation. "Don't worry, Maame, he has a whole list of things to do."

"Your daughter has graciously agreed to be my tour guide."

The revelation seemed to please Aunty Ama quite a bit. He'd only just met the woman, but Ty discovered he liked seeing her happy. It made him wonder how she'd react if the paternity of Patricia's baby became known to her. He hoped she would be forgiving of it, especially once he told her his intentions toward her daughter.

He hadn't raised the issue of marriage again, hoping a few days would give Patricia enough time to think about it and change her mind. This time, he wasn't taking no for an answer.

"Anyway," Patricia said, checking her time. "Maame, I think we should let Ty go to his hotel so he can rest."

"Hotel? No, no, no," her mother said. "Baaba, how can you bring a guest and send him to stay in a hotel? Didn't you say he's a friend of Naaki's fiancé? There's a *sofabed* in my room. You will sleep on it, and he can have your old room."

Patricia didn't look happy, and despite his desire to make her mother like him, he needed Patricia to like him more.

"Aunty Ama, it's not a problem at all, and I wouldn't want to impose."

She gave him a dismissive wave. "It's no imposition at all. You must stay with us. Baaba, tell him."

He looked at Patricia, who returned his stare with an icy glare.

"Yes, Ty. Why don't you stay?" she said.

He nodded his acceptance of the invitation, though at the back of his mind, he knew he'd have to make it up to Patricia.

⌀⌀⌀

Patricia stared helplessly at the scene unfolding before her—Maame looking at Ty as if he were the son she'd always wanted. Patricia wished she could say Ty had charmed her mum, turned her into something unrecognizable, but sadly this came as no surprise. What had her thrown for a loop was how fate had intervened to ensure nothing went as planned this past week. Her mother wasn't even supposed to be at home at this time. Wednesday mornings were market days for her mother, and Patricia had factored it into her plans. Otherwise, she wouldn't even have risked bringing Ty anywhere near her neighborhood.

She could only imagine what a mess fate would create if she didn't take back the reins of her life. But how? Could she stay in her mum's room for the next four days without the older woman finding out about the baby or who the father was? How did she make sure her mother didn't start having expectations of some future her daughter might have with the father of her child?

The wall clock chimed, noisily announcing the time. *Noon.*

"You must both be hungry," her mum said.

Great. Patricia stood with her mum. Hopefully, while helping with lunch, she'd manage to convince her mother to let Ty go to the hotel. As for Ty, maybe a few moments alone would help him think about the predicament he'd put her in.

"Oh, no. Stay with your friend," her mother said.

Patricia wanted to roll her eyes and pout like a teenager, but it wouldn't help. She lowered herself back on the chair and waited until her mother had left the room. She turned to Ty, but he spoke first.

"I like your mother."

"Of course, you do." Her voice sounded more scathing than she'd intended, probably a direct result of her insides being wound as tight as the old twin-bell alarm clock her mother refused to upgrade. "Everyone likes my mum." *Except Paapa.* "She's friendly, kind, chatty—a little pushy, frankly. She's stubborn and doesn't know when to quit."

Ty smiled. "Hey, enjoy her. You've got a mother who loves you. That's a lot more than I had."

His words had the same effect on her anger as cold water on embers. He'd never talked about his mother. She knew his dad had passed away and he'd grown up with an aunt, but the one time his mother had come up in conversation, it had been shoved under the too-personal rug.

"After my dad died, my mother took off. We would have ended up in the foster system if my aunt hadn't taken us in. It wasn't fun and games, though. She'd lost her husband a couple of years earlier and had five kids of her own. We had to take jobs as soon as we were old enough to wash cars or bus tables just to keep us going."

He stood, taking a few steps, and then stopping. "My aunt loved us. I wouldn't be where I am today if it weren't for her, but my mom's rejection still stung. If my own mother couldn't log another few years until her son turned eighteen, then—"

He stopped, cleared his throat. Hearing the rawness of the emotion in his voice, her own feelings of hurt and exasperation receded to the background. She wanted to say something but had no idea what to say. Luckily, she didn't have to, because he continued.

"Don't ever take her for granted."

She shook her head, still struggling to find her voice. Now that she knew why Ty had enjoyed the little chat with her mother, she couldn't go ahead with her plan to send him off to a hotel. She'd just have to find a way of ensuring her mother never discovered the real relationship between her and Ty. Talk about being caught between the fire and the frying pan.

He faced her. "Look, I know you didn't want me to

meet your mother, but if it's any consolation, I don't think it went badly at all, unless…" His eyes narrowed with suspicion and his brows creased. "You said she wouldn't like me because I got you pregnant."

Her heart pounded. "Will you keep your voice down?"

"You haven't told her it's me, have you?"

She swallowed. "Something like that."

He chuckled. Patricia hadn't heard a scarier sound, because she had no idea what would come next. Her pulse raced as he approached her. Wordlessly, he came to sit by her.

"Does she even know about the baby?"

Dammit! "You're pushy."

"I'll take that as a no." He took her hand. "Look at me."

Letting out a pent-up breath, she raised her eyes to meet his gaze.

"I know she probably treats everyone nicely, but I did like her, and I'd love for her not to hate me. Not until—"

"Baaba," her mother called from the kitchen, interrupting their conversation.

"Not until what?" she urged.

He shook his head, as if rethinking his words. "Don't worry about it. Your secret is safe with me."

Her mother called again.

"Yes, Ma. *Me re ba*," Patricia answered, then to Ty, she said, "Excuse me."

As she stood, her mind lingered on those two words. *Not until.*

Not until what?

∞∞∞

For a meal prepared in less than forty minutes, her

mother had outdone herself. Seated on one long side of the table-for-six, Patricia surveyed the wealth of food before them. She couldn't imagine how on earth her mother had whipped up Jollof rice, ripe plantain and beans stew—commonly called red-red—and Patricia's favorite, boiled yam and garden egg sauce prepared in an earthenware pot. Ty would certainly love this variety of local foods.

"Wow, Maame," she said. "Have you acquired a cooking elf?"

Aunty Ama beamed. "I had already prepared some of the food this morning. I had to go to the market yesterday, since we had little food in the house, and I knew you were coming today."

Well played, universe or fate or whatever. Well played.

"Baaba, why don't you check if Menaesi is awake?"

Patricia excused herself from the table and went to find her grandaunt. As she raised her hand to knock on the door, it opened. She wondered if Menaesi had "seen" her coming.

"Lunch is ready," Patricia said.

"Where do you think I'm going?" Menaesi said with a twinkle in her eyes. "I don't need help, you know."

Smiling, Patricia stepped aside for her grandaunt to pass. For an octogenarian, her grandaunt was in great shape, still able to get around on her own. Although the doctor had recommended a walking stick, Menaesi had ditched it, saying it made her look like an old lady.

As the old woman moved past her, she stopped and searched Patricia's eyes for several seconds. She touched Patricia's face then placed a finger on the tender flesh at the base of her neck.

"I see."

Oh come on! Patricia knew some older women alleged to have a sixth sense about pregnancy. Some claimed they could spot pregnancy even before a test could detect it. Something about seeing babies' feet on a pregnant woman's forehead.

"What do you see, Menaesi?"

The woman only smiled. "Even with the best of intentions, people make mistakes," she said. "Take heart. In the end he will make you happy."

O-kaay. Had the old woman just predicted her baby's sex or had she been referring to Ty? Patricia shook her head. *Ridiculous.* She'd rounded out a little, but she wasn't showing yet, so no way could her grandaunt be talking about the baby.

Without another word, the old woman started walking away.

It took only seconds for Patricia to decide not to play dumb and risk Menaesi blurting out her suspicions over lunch.

"Wait!"

Menaesi turned.

"Maame doesn't know. I'd like to tell her myself."

"It's not my place to tell her, child."

"Thank you," Patricia said, and for the first time since arriving in Cape Coast, she felt like she'd begun to regain control of the situation.

Chapter 9

After lunch, they'd sat around the table and continued the conversation until Patricia's mother and great aunt decided to retire to their rooms. Patricia wanted some fresh air, so Ty suggested the porch.

Gazing at the relatively quiet street, Ty could honestly count today as one of the happiest of his life. Sure, he'd traveled extensively, had even done business in Asia and South America where many people were just as friendly as in Ghana. In none of those countries had he experienced the same overwhelming sense of belonging currently pulsing within him. Or maybe it simply had to do with the company.

He glanced at Patricia, who sat on an easy chair fiddling with a beaded bracelet on her left arm. It appeared to have come undone, and she busied herself securing it in place. A smile came to his lips as he watched her dainty hands at work. They seemed so small in comparison with his, deceptively small, because whenever she laid them on him the effect was always overwhelming.

As though sensing his gaze, she looked up. "*Maaba okwεo me?*"

"That doesn't sound like Akan."

She raised her brows. "I can't believe you were able to tell the difference. It's Ga, spoken by the people of Accra, and it means why are you looking at me?"

What he said next, might have sounded silly, but no less heartfelt. "Thank you."

She raised a brow. "For what?"

"For letting me stay."

"My mum insisted," she said. "You were there."

"We both know you could have convinced her to change her mind if you wanted, and if you'd insisted I leave, I'd have done it without hesitation."

She shrugged. "Yes, well. I figured you'd enjoy the food here better. Besides, what kind of maid of honor would I be if I didn't look out for the best man?"

He chuckled. *Touché.*

"Plus, if you knew my mother, you'd realize when she sets her mind on something, she gets it."

"Looks like the apple didn't fall very far from the tree."

"I don't get what I want all the time."

"Nobody does." He shrugged. "Besides, you're getting Beauty by Patricia."

"I am."

"Speaking of which, have you considered getting a partner and setting it up as a joint venture or even a limited liability company?"

Her brows creased, and she shook her head. "To be honest, no. Either option would mean I won't be in control of my company. One of the several reasons I started working for myself is to have full decision-making responsibility. I don't need someone second-guessing my choices."

He'd figured as much but pressed on in a bid to plant the seed in her mind. "You don't necessarily have to cede control. It will all depend on the agreement you sign with the person. For example, you could have a silent or limited partner and you will still be the managing partner. On the plus side, you'll get someone to share the risk."

She looked pensive for a moment. "Who would I ask?"

"Anyone who believes in your idea."

"I'll think about it." She smiled briefly then became quiet, contemplative. "There's something I've desired for a long time and never got."

She didn't have to say what—or whom. He recognized the pain and longing in her voice. "Your dad."

She nodded, raising sad eyes at him. "He was the perfect dad, you know. I was only six and a half, yet I remember him. When I turned five, he took me to the stadium to watch a football match." She snorted. "He'd hoped for a boy."

A few moments elapsed while she kept her gaze on the street. "On his last day with us, I remember feeling something was wrong. He let me skip school and my dad was all about his daughter getting an education."

At least the guy had done something right. He shook his head. As bad as he thought his pain had been, he realized she'd had it worse. She'd seen what it was like to have the love of a father. He, on the other hand, didn't get a mother with much of a maternal instinct. Even before abandoning them, she'd been a firm believer in the philosophy of sparing the rod and spoiling the child." He'd loved her anyway, and when she'd left, he'd been older.

Man up, get over it, and comfort her.

He knew she wouldn't let him, though. Not when her mother could walk out here any moment. Instead, he reached out and squeezed her shoulder. Somehow that didn't cut it. He stood, grabbed her hands, and gave a gentle tug. She let him pull her up. He didn't hug her like he wanted to. Instead, he entwined their fingers and pulled her only as close as he dared while keeping a decent space between them, in case they had an audience.

"You know what I don't get?" she said. "How a man can love someone and still leave. Or how a person can make a promise he has no intention of keeping."

Ty paused, trying to come up with a good response, but he didn't get the chance before she spoke again.

"My mum says he loved me, and the truth is, I believe it, which is what makes it so hard to understand. He actually told me he was going somewhere, but he promised to come back." She looked at him. "I wish he hadn't told me. I wish he'd just left instead of making me spend every day for years waiting for his return."

"Trish, I can never hope to explain why your dad left or why he never returned, but I promise you not all men are like him."

She gave a snort. "Just the ones who matter, right?"

Her words were like little darts discharged at close range for maximum impact, but Ty didn't flinch, knowing it was her pain talking. *I'm here,* he wanted to say. *Don't I matter?* The words even rose to the tip of his tongue, but he bit them back.

Instead, he whispered, "We're both damaged goods. That's why we're perfect together."

He'd half expected her to detangle herself from his grasp, but she smiled, and he could have sworn she leaned in a tad. The browns of her eyes intensified with emotions that reached into him, filled him.

"Marry me, Trish."

She stiffened, but he noted she didn't disentangle their hands. Her eyes bored into his for the longest time, and he could almost see the wheels of her mind turning, searching…for a reason to say yes? On the one hand, he understood her uncertainty. Objectively, proposing to a woman only three and a half months after meeting her seemed a little desperate. Especially when most of that time had been spent apart. When he'd first proposed, doing the right thing had been a significant part of his reason. However, in the past couple of days, everything had changed somehow. There was no uncertainty on his part. He wanted this, wanted her, wanted what they could be together. The evidence was damning—heart pounding, breath catching, palms beginning to sweat. Oh, yeah. He had it bad.

Still, she hadn't spoken a word.

"I know you're scared, but have you stopped to think," he continued. "I'm probably one of very few people who know exactly how you feel and what you're afraid of."

"Ty…"

He saw the doubt in her eyes. "I know what it's like to be abandoned by a parent, which is why you have to trust I'd never do it to you or our child."

She withdrew her hands, moved to the railing where she gazed straight ahead. He followed her, leaned backward against the railing so he could look more directly at her. His hands felt heavy at his sides, wanting to touch her. He shoved them into his pockets, just to give them something to do.

"It's not that I'm not tempted. I look at my married friends or those getting married, and sometimes I want to have someone pledge me a lifetime together." She glanced at him. "But I'm not going to marry for the sake of marrying or doing the right thing."

Ty exhaled sharply. As long as they were dialoguing, he could be confident she'd come around to his way of thinking.

"I'm not asking you to, but don't you think maybe you're saying no for the sake of saying no?"

She frowned, looked at him as if he'd asked her the chicken and egg question.

"You think I enjoy you asking and me refusing? I don't, and I wish you'd stop asking, so we can figure out how to make the best of things for our child."

"What if the 'best of things' isn't good enough?"

She didn't respond.

"Has it occurred to you that marriage in itself may not be bad? It's what you do with it that determines how it goes?"

"You sound like such a romantic."

"No, I'm being real. Tell me you weren't happy when your parents were together. I know I was, but of course I had no idea my dad was the glue holding our family together. My mom had just been making the best of things, so the moment she got an out, she took it."

He cupped her cheek, allowing himself to savor the softness as he caressed her. A part of him sensed they'd made progress, but at this pace, they'd probably still be talking by the time the baby came along. Being a man of action, he didn't want to talk shop when he could do.

"Honey, there's one thing about me you haven't grasped. I'm a man of my word." He kept his voice neutral, because he didn't want to come off as a bully but needed to make his stand clear. "When my mom left, I promised I'd never do what she did to a child of mine. I don't intend to break that vow, so I'm going to keep asking until you say yes."

∽❃∽

Why the hell did he want to marry her?

The question had plagued Patricia since yesterday afternoon when Ty had promised to wear her down with his persistence. She'd offered him a free pass, a deal many guys would take and run with. The way he went on about it, you'd think he'd developed feelings for her, which might make sense, except she knew he didn't. He couldn't.

Another thing he couldn't do was make her change her mind. He had no idea what he was trying to get himself into, so it was up to her to save him.

Something bumped into her, yanking her out of her thoughts. She realized her mother had nudged her.

"Baaba, are you all right? You haven't heard a word I've said."

Patricia grappled with her subconscious, attempting to fish out a memory of anything her mother had said over the past few minutes. Nothing. She couldn't think past the rankling potpourri of smells, a melee of drugs and heavy-duty disinfectant that didn't let you forget for a second you were in a hospital. They waited in a long queue to see her mother's regular doctor, and Patricia already anticipated spending most of the day here. Typical Thursday at the hospital. Tomorrow being the last working day of the week would be worse.

Normally her mother would complain about the queue, everything wrong with the healthcare system, and the stench while Patricia tried to ignore it. Today, though, the hospital smell had caused two or three unwanted gag reflexes, which had taken a serious Oscar-worthy performance on her part to hide. She'd been lucky so far with the nausea. It only attacked in the mornings and stayed away as long as she ate an orange every couple of hours.

She swallowed, forcibly directing her mind to her mother's accusation. "Sorry, Maame. I was just thinking, that's all."

"About your *friend*?"

Patricia chuckled. Though, speaking in Fante, her mother had said "friend" in English, which meant a whole lot more than a mere friend.

"He's not my 'friend.'"

Her mind flashed on images of some of her passion-inflamed nights with Ty. *Lovers, not friends*. Then again, since lovers had "love" in it, maybe it really wasn't better.

"He's Thane's friend, and I'm only being nice to him because we have to work together on the wedding."

Her mother smiled. "I've been a young woman in love before, you know."

"Maame, I'm not a young woman in love."

"Deny it all you want, but I've seen the way you look at each other." Her mother seemed pleased with herself as she winked. "Or should I say the way he looks at you, while you pretend not to be looking at him."

Okay, Patricia obviously had to work on that, but right now she needed to get her mother off her case, and she knew one sure-fire way to do so. "Maame, did you remember to take your medicine this morning?"

Her mother scrunched her face. "Yes, I did, and don't think I don't know what you're doing."

"I don't know what you're talking about." Making air quotes, Patricia added, "You forget to take your medicine too often, even after herbal treatments clearly didn't do anything to help."

Her mother shook her head as if Patricia were to be pitied.

"All those drugs that doctors like to pump us with, if you take time to read the information, you will see they all have horrible side effects. Herbal medicine, on the other hand, is natural. It takes time to work but gets to the root of the problem."

She paused the lecture as a nurse came to announce a

list of names for patients to move to an inner room. The queue moved seven places. They were now fourth in line for the inner room.

As they settled in their new seats, her mother continued, "Young children of today. Your problem is lack of patience and respect for tradition."

Here we go. Patricia resisted the urge to roll her eyes.

"Even your friend, Ty, appreciates the value of our traditions and customs, though he's not Ghanaian."

"Maame, I've told you, Ty is—"

"Not your friend," her mum interrupted, gracing Patricia with a sweet smile. "You keep saying that, and I'm telling you I don't believe you."

Patricia threw her arms up in exasperation. "Why are we even talking about him?"

Her mother gave her what Patricia had once termed a mother-knows-best smile and proceeded to focus her attention on an overhead television set showing a Nigerian movie.

Patricia sat back with a sigh. Despite her last words, her mind went straight to Ty. What was he up to? She'd worried about leaving him home with Menaesi, but he'd insisted he didn't mind. It was a preferred alternative to having him tag along on their hospital trip. No matter how much her mother liked Ty, there was no way she'd want him here for her hospital appointment. He'd stayed behind to keep Menaesi company while they'd arranged for a young woman from next door to check in on them in case the old woman, in particular, needed help.

After they returned from the hospital, he'd agreed to continue the work they'd started on Beauty by Patricia, but she might rather lure him out of the house. If anyone suggested it, she'd deny, deny, deny, but she kind of missed having him all to herself.

❡❡❡

The solution appeared simple, yet so diabolical, Ty had spent the afternoon going back and forth on his preparedness to take such a step. After yesterday's talk with Patricia, it had hit home that he needed to do more than keep asking until she said yes. He hadn't known the answer to his predicament, nor had he expected to arrive at it quickly, so when he'd woken up this morning, he'd decided to do what he did whenever faced with a problem— put it aside for a while and return a little later with "new" eyes.

After Patricia and her mother left for the hospital, he'd spent the rest of the morning catching up on emails, including one from his sister reminding him to bring back a souvenir from Africa, and addressing urgent client matters. After several long minutes on the phone reassuring a couple of his top clients that taking a rare six weeks off didn't constitute the beginning of a nervous breakdown, he did something he'd never done before.

He'd spent an hour on the internet searching for things like "How to get her to say yes," and "the perfect proposal." God, how he'd have ribbed any of his friends if he'd caught them doing this.

It was well past noon before he decided to take a break. He became aware of some activity in the house and guessed Patricia's great aunt had come out of her room. At eighty-something, the old woman, like many of her era, didn't know her exact date of birth. For official purposes, they'd selected a date, which she didn't remember. He'd discovered births and deaths in the old days had been marked by events rather than calendars—a piece of trivia that made him even more eager to discover the hidden treasures of Africa.

He'd enjoyed Menaesi's tales of days gone by during

supper last night, so when he'd switched off his iPad and headed to the sitting room to sit with her, he'd hoped for more of the same. He'd gotten a whole lot more.

She'd been full of stories and even a few interesting ideologies about the unanswered questions in the universe. Patricia had warned him about the old woman's eccentricities—i.e. she was clairvoyant—so he shouldn't really have been surprised when she revealed her knowledge about the pregnancy and even the fact that the baby was his. He'd found himself opening up to her, telling her about his intentions toward her great niece.

That's how the conversation about marriage started—what it meant in general, what it signified in Ghana, how it shouldn't be entered into lightly not just because it bound two people to each other for life but because in this part of the world, marriage also united families. You couldn't just elope, and divorce could only be achieved by an agreement of the families.

Then she'd handed him the solution to his predicament on a proverbial silver platter. However, like every easy fix, there was a catch.

Standing at the gate, now, people-watching, he played the conversation over and over in his head as he awaited Patricia's return from the hospital with her mother. Should he discuss it with her or simply do it? The first might meet opposition. He snorted. What was he saying? The first *would* meet opposition from her, and the second would be cruel—cruel enough for her to hate him, at least for a while. Eventually, though, she'd forgive him. She'd have to, once she understood he'd done it in the interest of their child. The end would justify the means.

He hoped.

Chapter 10

Ty had read the history and knew of the morbid legacy of the Cape Coast Castle, the stately edifice which once represented the last stop, a point of no return, for men and women sold into slavery before they made the journey across the Atlantic Ocean. Built by the Swedish in the seventeenth century for the trade of gold and timber, the castle had changed owners many times in its history. Now under the stewardship of the Ghana Museums and Monuments Board, it attracted as much traffic today as it did in the seventeenth and eighteenth centuries, the reason this visit had been top priority on his trip.

They'd parked the car at a designated parking area a little distance away and made their way to the building on foot. From where they approached, the road was a gentle upward slope that made the castle appear even grander.

"It must have been something else in the seventeenth century."

Patricia nodded. "I'm sure some of these buildings weren't here at the time."

They met a short queue at the entrance where they paid a nominal admission fee. As they walked past the front desk, Ty paused and assimilated the significance of the moment.

Although his investigations into his ancestry had been inconclusive, Ty felt something…something that told him his roots might just be here.

Patricia stopped at his side and took his hand, as if recognizing the significance of the moment for him.

He let out a breath he'd been holding. "My ancestors may have passed through here."

She responded with a gentle squeeze of his hand.

They stepped into an open space in the middle of the castle, where all the other tourists had gathered.

"Good morning," a uniformed castle guide greeted, standing in front of the small crowd. "Welcome to Cape Coast Castle."

The guide started off with some housekeeping rules then went on to narrate the history of the castle, the various owners, the trade, and some trivia, some of which Ty had read prior to this visit.

The tour began at the museum, which housed an extensive collection of the branding irons and shackles used to confine human beings—his ancestors—and blue prints of the ships which took them away from life as they knew it. Ty had been taking pictures and filing away notes until the tour paused in the dungeons, chambers with two or three small holes providing minimal lighting.

"These rooms were filled with up to two hundred people at a time," the guide said solemnly.

Ty swore. Even with only twenty or so tourists, the walls seemed to be closing in on them. A chill ran up his spine as he tried to imagine the unthinkable acts that had gone on in here and the long journey to freedom that had culminated in him finding his way to this spot, at this time, with the one person in the world he'd have chosen to be here with.

"Spooky," someone whispered. "It's like the spirits of those who passed through here still haunt this place."

The tour moved to the women's quarters, a chamber just like the previous one except this one had a hatch, opening directly into the governor's office. At this point Ty's emotions threatened to overtake him with an irrepressible combination of indignation, sorrow, and a deep sense of loss.

Patricia touched him, claiming his attention. She had tears in her eyes, but she was taking photos with the camera he'd forgotten about at some point. He hadn't even realized when she'd prized it from his grasp.

The tour had been harrowing, but its completion felt like a rebirth for Ty. The theory had been a good place to begin but walking through the footsteps of those who'd passed through here had made his search complete somehow.

They returned to the open area where they began the tour, and their guide gave his final narration of how the castle came to be included on the UNESCO World Heritage list.

"Are you okay?" Patricia asked.

"I will be." He took in her still misty eyes. "Is this your first time here?"

She shook her head. "I've been here a couple of times before, but it's still hard to believe all those things happened."

As they exited, Ty's attention caught on a plaque embedded in the wall and paused to read the inscription.

IN EVERLASTING MEMORY
OF THE ANGUISH OF OUR ANCESTORS
MAY THOSE WHO DIED REST IN PEACE

MAY THOSE WHO RETURN FIND THEIR ROOTS
MAY HUMANITY NEVER AGAIN PERPETUATE
SUCH INJUSTICE AGAINST HUMANITY
WE, THE LIVING, VOW TO UPHOLD THIS

"Amen," he said.

He wrapped an arm around Patricia, and they stood there for a moment longer before proceeding out.

The Ghanaian society was relatively conservative, and public displays of affection were largely frowned on, so Ty waited until they reached the car before pulling Patricia into his arms and kissing her.

When they parted, she tossed a glance around, althhough her eyes danced. "What was that for?"

He pretended to think about it for a few seconds before answering, "For sharing this moment with me, for being the mother of my child, and most of all—" he kissed her again "—just because."

She giggled, a sound he wanted to continue being responsible for.

He opened the door for her. "Come on, we still have to go to Kakum."

ဗာၝ

Some people enjoyed driving. Patricia didn't, so the fact that Ty was handling his first driving in Ghana like a pro won him major points. He kept his eyes on the road, while nodding to R&B hits streaming from a radio station Patricia was unfamiliar with. In profile, his lashes appeared longer than she'd initially thought, which many of the female population of the world would think unfair. She knew, first hand, his eyelashes weren't the only attractive feature on him.

"You have a fine head," she said.

"What?" He darted a glance her way, a frown knitted through his brows. "How do you define a fine head?"

"Nicely shaped. Your forehead isn't too pronounced, and you've got a nice gentle slope at the back."

He chuckled. "Thank you. I think."

"If you were in line for chieftaincy, you'd be very happy about it."

"You pick kings based on the shape of their heads?"

She chuckled at his shock. "No, of course not, but stature is very important. A king must have a presence, command respect. All that good stuff, and a man with features that can be used against him isn't the preferred choice."

"What happens if the heir to the throne has an ugly head?"

"Maybe it's why we don't have a 'first in line' system of succession. Due to the matrilineal heritage of Akans, a king isn't succeeded by his own children, but by a maternal nephew, so there tends to be multiple candidates, all of equal standing, which means the king makers can afford to be a little picky."

"A little? They're disqualifying potential kings for having ugly heads."

"That's not what I said."

He laughed again. "God, I love Africa. I love how little things like that have implications and history."

Patricia shook her head at the generalized identifier, Africa, but made no comment.

"Come on, let's hear it."

"Hear what?"

"I saw the disapproval on your face."

"It's not disapproval," she said. "It's just that the continent is so diverse, it seems such a shame when the rest of the world bunches it all together like we're one country."

"Honey, believe me, I know the continent is diverse, but it doesn't negate what I said. Every corner of Africa has a rich heritage."

She conceded his point. "Sometimes, I'm tempted to believe that's what's holding the continent back. You know, too much culture and heritage, and too many protocols to be observed."

They became quiet for the stretch of a song, then in a soft voice second only to the gentleness of his tone when they made love, Ty spoke.

"You were right, you know."

"About what?"

"What you said about African-Americans and Africa."

She winced, remembering the last time the topic of African-Americans had come up. Did she really want to have this conversation?

"Africa is like an elusive dream, an ideal we can't attain, no matter how much we want to. For me, it's like a what-if situation. What if they'd never built Cape Coast castle? What if the traders had stuck with timber and spices? Would Africa be better off? Would we be better off?" He snorted. "You think we don't know we don't belong here?"

Patricia heard the pain in his voice but had no idea what she could say to soothe it.

He slowed down to take a turn, before speaking again. "I'll admit, we do take some things personal, but it's because we grow up in a system designed to remind us we don't belong, and we don't have the stuff you take for granted."

"Like what?"

"Your cultures and traditions."

"Didn't you hear me say those things may be holding us back?"

"I did, and you could be right, but, honey, it's something you have control over. You have the choice to make changes where you deem fit. We don't have that."

She didn't blame him. He had no idea how deep-seated some of these traditions were, and in some cases, what sort of rites and rituals went into making one little change. If she tried to outline them for him, the conversation would turn into a speech.

"When you serve someone water before you welcome him, you know where it comes from. You never have to wonder how different life might have been if your ancestors hadn't been taken."

He stopped, cleared his throat. She reached out and touched him. He glanced at her, his eyes burning with passion and determination.

"You were also wrong," he said, returning his gaze to the road. "This is not a passing fancy for me. My roots are on this continent, even if I don't exactly belong here."

She didn't know whether it was the words that struck a chord or the somber tone of his voice, but it made her want to cry and comfort him at the same time.

"You know what my mother said yesterday? She said I should be more like you, more interested in culture and tradition."

"She did?"

"It looks like you belong a lot more than you think."

"I certainly feel at home here."

"I'm glad you do, but you have opportunities, which we don't have over here, so I guess sometimes I find it odd to hear you say we've got it better."

The conversation continued in the same manner, lighthearted yet meaningful. By the time they reached their destination, Patricia had learned so much more about Ty. Not just the easy stuff, but some of his deepest desires, among them a yearning to belong. It drew her in and scared her at the same time. The first because she saw just how big a heart he had, and the second because, contrary to her initial impressions, Ty longed for a family. How hadn't she seen it before?

She'd assumed his insistence on marriage had more to do with his male ego than anything else. Could she have been wrong? Did Ty want a family with her? An image flashed through her mind of them as a family—Ty, her, a baby, a nice house...

She shook it off. This wasn't the time for daydreams. Maybe after he left, when she laid alone in bed missing his touch, she'd think about what could have been. When the baby kept her awake half the night, she'd allow herself to wonder what it would have been like to sleep knowing she had a dependable man at her side to tend to her and their little angel.

That was the problem. She couldn't depend on Ty. No matter what he said now, he might change his mind, because his life was in America, which wouldn't be changing anytime soon. For the sake of her child, she couldn't afford to dream about forever with Ty.

She forced the thoughts out of her mind. Today she wanted to be here with Ty. Cape Coast Castle had been emotional, and she hoped Kakum National Park would be the opposite.

She turned to him. "Ready?"

"Hell, yeah."

She chuckled.

They headed to the visitors' center to pay the admission fee and pick up a brochure. Just as with the castle, a tour guide welcomed them and proceeded to talk about the two main attractions—a guided tour through portions of the vast moist evergreen rainforest with hardwood trees over fifty meters tall, and a forty-meter high canopy walkway suspended between said trees.

Patricia had managed to avoid the canopy walkway during her first visit to Kakum National Park but looking at the excitement in Ty's eyes, she wondered if she'd succeed this time.

She didn't.

"Don't chicken out on me," he'd said. "I'll be right there with you."

An hour later, after their tour through the rain forest and a short rest, they walked up a steep trail to the hilltop where the canopy walk began. The initial landing was a hutted space with benches, Patricia gratefully sat on one to catch her breath. Ty preferred to stand akimbo taking measured breaths as if he'd only done warm ups. *Show off.*

In addition to the two staff who had guided them up the trail, there were two other staff in the hut. One of those they met in the hut gave a talk about the engineering behind the canopy walkway assuring tourists of the safety. Meanwhile, the other took a leisure walk about two yards into the first suspended bridge and bounced a couple times against the sides to assure everyone it was perfectly safe.

"Awesome," Ty said, facing her with a grin that would challenge any child on Christmas morning, as if expecting her to show the same level of excitement.

She managed a smile.

"You're not scared of heights, are you?"

She shook her head and winced. "Of course not," she stammered. "I just prefer my feet to be firmly on the ground."

Heights per se didn't make her nervous, but rather the fact that she'd be forty meters above the ground, walking on wooden planks held together by ropes. *Wire ropes are still ropes.*

"There are seven bridges with six rest stops in between," the park staff was saying. "You can change your mind after the first bridge, but once you cross to the second, you must finish the walk."

Okay, Patricia thought, there was an out. She could do the first, so she didn't completely spoil the fun for Ty. Besides, as one lady got on the first bridge, it seemed sturdy enough, and the woman who'd initially seemed nervous didn't appear scared at all.

"You okay?" Ty asked.

Patricia nodded, standing. *I can do this*.

They let people on one at a time waiting for the person to get about halfway across the first bridge before the next person followed, limiting it to a maximum of three people on the bridge at the same time. It seemed like a good system.

When it reached their turn, one of the men said, "Ladies first?"

"No," Patricia said. "He goes first."

Without hesitation, Ty stepped onto the bridge moving at a casual pace. Taking in a breath, Patricia followed, holding the sides in a death grip. *Okay, not so bad.* She continued gingerly, looking down at her feet. Before she knew it, she'd reached the first rest area, the last point where she could change her mind.

"That wasn't so bad, right?" Ty said.

Patricia shook her head. It hadn't been as bad as she'd imagined. Besides, when she looked at Ty and saw the grin on his face, she knew chickening out now would wipe off the grin and she kind of liked seeing it there.

Ty waited for the person on the next bridge to get onto the next rest stop before he went on. With a deep breath, Patricia abandoned the platform along with any hopes of turning back. Halfway in, she began to breathe easier, even dared to laugh at her earlier fears. She finally took her eyes off her feet to look around. *Wow*. At this altitude the view was stunning. The tree tops were so green, so lush, despite the dry January weather. Birds flittered around, the sight as colorful as a cartoon scene, except this was a hundred times more enchanting.

"Woohoo!" Ty screamed.

He had stopped in the middle, his hands raised above his head.

"Move," Patricia yelled.

Then the bridge started swaying. She heard a scream and froze. It took a moment to realize the scream had come from her. She looked back. Someone else had joined them on the bridge, which must have caused the sway.

Patricia maintained her death grip on the ropes and swallowed but her heart continued to pound. *Oh God, why did I agree to this?*

"Keep moving," someone said.

Shut up, she wanted to shout at the person, maybe even use an expletive while she was at it. Patricia tried to move, but her legs had suddenly assumed the weight of lead. Intellectually, she knew the bridge was sturdy enough for the three people, but intellect didn't reduce the shaking in her arms and legs.

Ty came to her side. One hand closed around her shoulder, the other holding on to the bridge. "Hey, it's okay."

His gentle touch and soothing voice cut through her fear, calming her several notches. How did he do that?

"I'm right here," he said.

His hand moved from her shoulder to cup her cheek, then his fingers trailed her jawline to her chin. He raised her face, and before she knew it, his lips captured hers. The kiss was brief, but when he pulled back, the trembling was gone, and she began to relax further.

"Heh, get a room!" someone yelled.

"You're wasting our time," came another protest.

Ty smiled graciously at them.

"Sorry, guys." He looked at her again. "You okay?"

She answered with a nod, taking in a deep breath. With that, Ty turned and led the way, making sure he remained no more than a few steps ahead of her. The swaying began again, and her heart pounded. She still held the ropes with white-knuckled grips, trying to mentally calm herself, but somehow it was Ty's solid presence a step ahead that kept her going.

She didn't like it at all. Since her father left, her mother had been the only person she could turn to, the only one she could allow to see her fears. If she wanted to be a good mother, provide the unwavering support her child needed, then she had to be able to rely on herself. She couldn't afford to have her mind create an association of comfort with any part of Ty. Not his voice, nor his presence, or his support.

Now if only she could transmit the message to her brain cells.

Chapter 11

They returned to an empty house. Today being Friday, Patricia's mother and grandaunt would have gone for Friday night church service. From the veranda, they could hear talking coming from inside.

"I thought you said they had somewhere to go."

"Church," she confirmed with a nod. "They leave the TV on to give the impression of someone being home."

A look of concern crossed Ty's face. "Is this a dangerous neighborhood?"

"Oh no, but no place is a hundred percent safe, and my mum prefers to err on the side of caution."

She jiggled the key a little. This spare had been cut after two of the three originals went missing, so it tended to stick in the lock.

"Do you need help with that?"

"There's a trick to it," she replied in lieu of a yes or no.

After her cry-baby scene at Kakum National Park,

she needed to reclaim some of her lost ego. Thankfully, the lock clicked. She sighed, opening the door.

"Ladies first," he said, stepping aside.

She chuckled at the allusion and entered. Once inside, she locked the door again.

"Strangely, locking the door never poses a problem," she said. "Are you hungry?"

She turned away from the door, and nearly smashed into Ty who stood right behind her. No traces of the playfulness from earlier in the day or the concern he'd shown just moments before reflected in his eyes. He gave her a full blown I-want-to-devour-you look and suddenly the room that could comfortably seat some twenty-something people felt too small.

Her breathing spiked, her pulse raced. Everything she'd ever felt for Ty came rushing at her all at once.

"I'm hungry for you," he said.

He closed the space between them, pinning her to the door with his body. A shudder stole through her at the contact. When his lips descended on hers, it was like nothing she'd ever felt—not even with Ty. Before today, his kiss had been like a fountain pouring on the parched lands of her lips, his touch like a flame singeing her skin, his tongue like a wand forged with the power to make her think of nothing except him.

Everything before today paled in comparison to the upheaval her body experienced now.

Whereas, usually, she remained conscious of her actions, giving as much as she got, teasing and enjoying being teased, this time she couldn't think, couldn't function. Passion burned within her like an unquenchable flame, leaving nothing untouched. With a hungered moan, she sank against the solid expanse of his chest, her hands roving every part of him she could touch in silent adoration of his sheer masculinity.

He released her lips, left her gasping as he tongued his way to her neck. His hand slipped underneath her blouse, found one of her breasts, and released it from the confines of her bra. Her nipples ached for his attention. He nipped the soft flesh of her neck with his teeth while stroking her nipple.

She moaned. "What are you doing to me?"

His only response was a groan before he pinched the hardened peak. She gasped, leaning into his touch. His other hand curled around her, firmly cupping her butt, holding her steady as he pressed his erection into her stomach. He tweaked her nipple again, harder. The combination of pain and pleasure birthed an ache in her core, had her fumbling with his belt buckle.

He foiled those plans by lifting her into his arms. She fell against him, wrapping her arms around his neck. He didn't kiss her as he carried her into the bedroom, but his intense and unwavering gaze left her breathless by the time he placed her on her old bed, surrounded by his scent.

He began to undress her, unbuttoning the blouse with painstaking deliberateness. She wanted to scream, urge him to hurry, but the torture of anticipation gave her such pleasure she continued to moan and whimper while he unfastened her top. Finally, the last button came undone and he slid open her blouse. He cupped her breasts, one already released the other still confined.

He caressed them until her nipples were hard, aching peaks.

"I want your lips," she begged, unsure she'd gotten her meaning across, but that was the extent of her current vocabulary.

Thankfully, he understood and lowered his mouth onto her nipple.

"Oh, Ty," she whispered, cradling his head.

After a moment, he undid the bra and paid attention to her other breast before moving down, caressing her, turning her into a whimpering mass of pleasures. He, on the other hand, appeared to be the model of control, his breath barely a notch heavier than usual. However, as he kneaded a trail down to her jeans, she felt the discrete trembling of his hands. When he reached her jeans, his gaze slid up to find hers as he rid her of the garment, followed by her panties. She now lay before him naked.

He pulled back as if admiring his handiwork. Then, staring into her eyes, he began to take off his T-shirt and then proceeded to remove his jeans and briefs together.

Patricia's eyes devoured his magnificence, and the ache in her core became full blown. Kneeling on the bed, he spread her legs, exposing her womanhood to his sight.

"Beautiful," he said.

Patricia held her breath. Normally, he'd whisper a command, make her tell him how he affected her, what she wanted him to do to her or tell her what he intended doing to her, but right now neither of them spoke, yet they had never been more in sync. She was more aroused than ever. If he didn't take her now, she'd come just from the intensity of his gaze, which would suck, because she wanted him inside her.

She wanted him to sink deep inside, fill and brand her, then as she floated into heaven, she wanted him to pour himself into her like the night he'd left her a piece of himself and taken a bit of her soul in exchange.

He lowered his weight onto her, then as he took her lips in a possessive kiss, he gave her what she yearned for—him, all of him, buried to the hilt. Her gratified cry mingled with his tortured one as they began to move in perfect unison. Joy burst inside her. She was conscious of nothing, not even breathing. If she died now, she wouldn't care. She doubted she'd even notice.

"Ty," she breathed. "You are…"

Wonderful. Exquisite.

"This is…"

Amazing. Heavenly.

"I know, honey," he whispered.

Her climax approached, a sumptuous sensation, enveloping her, filling her, casting her into weightlessness until she tipped over, soared into an otherworldly realm where nothing existed but her, and her pleasure…and the one who brought her there. As she began to drift back down on a joyous cloud, he met her as his release hit, renting out of him violent shakes as his seed hit her inner walls.

They continued to hold each other for several long minutes, surrounded by the sounds of their mingled breaths. The weightlessness hadn't lifted, and Patricia continued to bask in it. His arms tightened around her and his lips touched her forehead. She shuddered.

I think I'm falling for you. She didn't know if she'd said it, but frankly, right at that moment, she didn't have it in her to care.

"T?"

Ty's voice, as soft as a caress, wrapped around her, cozy as a blanket on a rainy day.

"Hm?"

"Thank you for today."

"My pleasure."

With a sigh of pure contentment, she snuggled closer. *Medɔfo.* The word swirled around in her mind and shut her eyes, welcoming sleep.

ↄ⃝ↄ⃝ↄ⃝

Ty was doing it again. Watching her sleep. He thought he'd known what it felt like to have her in his arms, to taste her lips, to be consumed by her, intoxicated with her essence. He'd been dead wrong, because their lovemaking tonight defied description—at least he hadn't been able to find the words. He only knew what he felt— tonight Patricia had given herself over completely to his possession and, in so doing, she'd reached into him and touched his very soul. Tonight, she became his woman. He wanted to shout it to the whole world, but he knew the world would have to wait. First, there was her family.

The thought brought him crashing back to earth. He couldn't let them find her in bed with him. Not until he and Patricia had come clean about everything. He made himself a promise to do so before they returned to Accra in the morning. After tonight, he had a feeling convincing Patricia wouldn't be a problem.

He leaned in and kissed her lightly on the lips. "Trish?"

She mumbled something unintelligible and went on sleeping.

A smile touched his lips as he kissed her again. "Wake up."

He continued giving her light pecks until she started kissing him back. When they parted, he was hard as a rock. He took her hand, placed it on his erection, and sucked in a breath at the sharp jolt invading him at the contact.

"See what you do to me?"

She gave him a sleepy smile and started rubbing him. He groaned and closed his eyes savoring every ounce of pleasure she evoked. *She has to get up now*. He shoved the thought from his mind and concentrated only on the feel of her soft palms on his engorged member. However, the pesky voice of reason persisted. They'd fallen asleep nearly an hour ago, and her mother and grandaunt should be home soon. He couldn't let them find Patricia with him like this. Not that he wasn't proud to be with her or to be found with her, but he knew she'd be mortified, so with a reluctant grunt, he placed his hand on hers, restraining her.

You must get dressed. That's what he'd meant to say, what he should have said, but when her eyes locked on his, they relinquished him of rational thought. He touched her face, stroking her cheek. Her eyes were dilated even though sleep still lingered in their depths.

"You're beautiful."

She smiled and whispered, "Thank you."

She brought her hand to his chest, paying particular attention to his nipples as she stroked them each in turn. He groaned, lying back. At this rate, he'd be begging her to spend the night with him.

"What's the meaning of *medofo*?"

"Do you mean, *Medɔfo*?" She gave him a curious look. "It means 'my love.' Who taught you that?"

"You said it before drifting off to sleep."

He couldn't have predicted what happened next. She pushed away from him. The next moment she got out of bed and started gathering her clothes.

"It's not possible," she said.

"What do you mean? You did say it."

Her leg kept slipping in her rush to wear her jeans. She hadn't even bothered to put on her panties first. He held her by the shoulders, stopping her.

"What are you afraid of?"

"I'm not afraid of anything." She jerked out of his grip and resumed her efforts at putting on her jeans, succeeding in slipping one leg in.

"Look at me, Trish."

She managed to put her second leg through and tugged the jeans all the way up, securing the buttons. As she slipped on her blouse, he caught her, once again halting her efforts as she attempted to button up. He pulled her into his arms. She went rigid, clutched her underwear between them like a shield.

"Tell me tonight wasn't different."

Her stance didn't change. "I need to go."

"Not until you admit it."

She averted her eyes, and he watched the play of various emotions on her face. She sighed, looking back at him. "Fine," she said. "Tonight was amazing, but you can't hold me accountable for anything I said in the throes of passion. Nothing has changed."

"How can you say that?"

She squirmed out of his grip. "This romantic notion you have of us and the baby living happily ever after is just a fantasy. You, of all people, should know."

"We're good for each other, Trish."

"For how long?"

She might as well have slapped him in the face. Clearly, she hadn't heard anything he'd said all this while. She may have listened, argued, but she hadn't really heard him. Did she want to?

"Do you think this is an act I'm putting on? Do you honestly believe there'll ever be a day I won't want to be there for you? For our child?"

She looked at him, and the combination of fire and ice in her eyes staggered him. "We cannot get married, so stop asking. Stop trying to fill my head with hope and high expectations of a life together."

"What's so wrong with a life together?"

"You don't get it, do you?" she asked.

"Explain it to me."

"I won't *need* you!"

Delivered individually, her words pierced him like a stab from a jagged knife. He reared back, realizing he needed to put up a shield against her darts.

Reining in his emotions, he took in a deep breath. "You're carrying my child, and you will not keep me away from my flesh and blood, so how about I stop asking and just take?"

His words took her aback. "What's that supposed to mean?"

"We *are* getting married," he said.

She laughed. "Good luck with that."

Undeterred, Ty went on. "I don't need luck. You see, yesterday I discovered something interesting."

Her smile dimmed, and she frowned. "What?"

He didn't get right to the point. He set the stage, so he could watch her reaction as he doled his own dose of reality.

"Ghanaian marriages are more about the family than the individual." He took one step closer to her. "The traditional ceremony is about gift-giving, a general expression of gratitude to the girl's parents for raising a gem of a woman, and a demonstration of the groom's ability to cater for his wife, which needless to say, I can do."

"So? I gave you all of that information."

He took another step, and she flinched, but didn't otherwise budge.

He delivered the last blow. "Here's the bit you didn't tell me. You can't marry without your family's consent, but they can marry you off without yours."

He heard the sharp intake of breath, saw the shock in her eyes, the disbelief that he'd actually spoken the words.

Yet, his infuriatingly stubborn woman held her head high and tried to school her expression, dared to call his bluff.

"That's ridiculous."

No smile, he noted.

"Is it, honey?" One final step brought him within

inches of her and her façade began to crumble. "Then why are you suddenly all tensed up?"

ⓔⓈⓔⓈ

Patricia attempted to speak, but her throat constricted and all that came out was a choking sound. His eyes burned with dangerous intent. What the hell had Menaesi told him and how did she undo it before intent became action?

Swallowing seemed to ease the tightness in her throat. "This is the twenty-first century. You can't do that."

"Are you sure?"

She didn't respond, because, in fact, he could. It was an archaic tradition, one that was all but abandoned, but not illegal since the law recognized customary marriage rules. She wasn't a traditionalist, but, contrary to her mother's belief, she did respect tradition, and she knew if Ty performed the necessary rites and her family accepted him as her husband, she'd have to submit to it.

"You wouldn't," she finally said. "I may not know everything about you, but I believe you're the last person who'd force a woman to marry him."

"You're right." He didn't give her time for any false sense of relief before he added, "You don't know everything about me, and you have no idea what I'd do for my kid."

To Patricia's mortification, when she opened her mouth to deal him an appropriate retort, her lips trembled, and tears shot to her eyes. She turned and ran out...

Smack into her mother.

Heat blazed Patricia's face as she desperately pulled her blouse to hide her naked chest. Her mother's gaze dropped to the vicinity of Patricia's stomach, her look of utter shock confirming she'd heard a good deal of her daughter's conversation with Ty. But it was the disappointment in her mother's eyes that made Patricia's shame complete.

"Baaba," It wasn't quite a gasp, but surprise registered in her eyes, briefly, as she returned her gaze to meet Patricia's. "Is everything all right?"

Leave it to her mother to ask a question like that when everything was clearly not all right.

Patricia managed a clipped, "Everything is fine."

She hadn't inherited her mother's ability to stay calm in situations where anyone else would be screaming their heads off. It didn't mean her mother couldn't be a lioness when she needed to be. No doubt her astute eyes had assessed the situation and summed up that nothing untoward had happened here.

It didn't minimize Patricia's mortification. Or her eagerness to get out of there before she started crying in earnest. She rushed past her mother and sought solace in the bedroom.

Chapter 12

Patricia leaned against the door, her heart still pounding from the double whammy of her argument with Ty and the encounter with her mother. The tears she'd hidden from Ty flowed freely as confused emotions roiled inside. Her mind reeled with the echo of his words, but her body continued to buzz with the remnants of sensations he'd evoked in her.

She should be worrying about her next conversation with her mother, preparing the right answers for all the questions she'd no doubt have. Instead, as she stepped away from the door and tossed her panties and bra on her valise, she thought about Ty's hands when they'd undressed her.

She shrugged the blouse off her shoulders, and as the light fabric feathered down her still sensitive skin, she fingered the planes and dips where Ty's tongue had licked and teased. *Dammit.* She should be hating him right now, formulating a plan of attack in case he made good on his threat to go behind her back and marry her.

Would he really do it? Surely not. Yet his words echoed in her mind, telling her otherwise. *You don't know everything about me.* She sucked in a breath. Even stuck in her head, the memory of his voice had an electric effect on her insides. She tried to think about something else, but her mind refused to comply. *You have no idea what I'd do for my kid.*

Did that include never leaving his kid's mother?

She chided herself. It was bad enough she'd begun falling for him. She didn't need to compound the problem by wishing for impossible things. Even if she threw caution to the wind and went with his crazy idea of getting married, she knew she'd regret it. More importantly, *he* would regret it someday. Whatever fascination he had now would fade and he'd want out.

After seeing the extent of his effect on her when her emotions were even a teeny bit involved, she knew if she let him in, it would only be a matter of time before she fell completely for him and when he left, she'd be crushed.

Good thing she hadn't fully fallen for him yet. She still had time to withdraw. *Perspective.* That's what she needed, and she knew exactly how to trigger it. She glanced at her mother's bedside alarm clock. *Nine-Thirty.* Naaki should still be awake. Hopefully, she wasn't with Thane, because Patricia needed to talk. A conversation with her best friend would give her perspective and calm her agitation. Better to do it now, she thought, before her mother finally came to have the conversation Patricia dreaded.

Searching around for her bag, it took only a few seconds to remember where she'd last had it—in Ty's temporary room. Heart sinking, she contemplated her options. She needed to speak to Naaki, but was she ready to face Ty again tonight?

☙❧

Ty bowed his head, silently cursing himself for losing his cool. What the hell had he been thinking, attacking Patricia like that? Making her cry? Especially when he'd already decided not to pursue that option. He'd had every good intention when he'd talked about the future, but her scathing words had struck him in the chest, sunk in, and twisted his insides into a mass of emotions and he'd lashed out.

He'd probably derailed any progress he might have made with her. Worse, her mother had heard everything. He cursed again, remembering Patricia's disheveled state as she'd stormed out, her blouse unbuttoned, clutching her underwear and shoes, teary-eyed in the wake of their argument…

None of it looked good. Even in the US it wouldn't go down well with most parents, so in a culture where honor and codes of conduct weren't taken lightly, his screw up must be phenomenal.

He took in a deep breath. *Time to take responsibility.* Exhaling, he headed out.

He found Aunty Ama in the living room, huddled in an armchair staring ahead of her. He stopped, bit back yet another expletive. He'd hoped to find Patricia first, make sure she was okay before facing her mother. He could only imagine what Aunty Ama thought of him now, after he'd not only impregnated her daughter but had the nerve to make love with her under her mother's roof. When Patricia had run out, he'd heard her mother's reaction. No further conversation had ensued. It may not have sounded like much of a scene, but he knew exactly how it had looked and he hated that Patricia had faced her mother alone.

However, Aunty Ama sat here and he had to face her

too. He remembered what Patricia had said about her mother's condition, about keeping her stress levels down.

As he approached, she raised her gaze. For several seconds she seemed to stare past him, then her eyes refocused on him. If she was angry, she didn't show it. This concerned him, because it meant the conversation could go in any direction. Anger, he could calm; pain, he could ease; disappointment, he could fix, but schooled diplomacy could get tricky. Or maybe his mistake had been to think she'd be as easy to read as her daughter.

He pointed to a seat. "May I sit?"

Her brows creased. She didn't answer for several seconds, but then she heaved a sigh and nodded. He sat with his hands linked on his lap, head held low, a posture of humility. An apology seemed to be the best place to start.

"Aunty Ama, I'm truly sorry," he said.

He didn't qualify it, because if he tried, it might not sound like an apology at all. He had no remorse about his feelings for Patricia, nor did he regret the amazing sex they'd just had or the fact that she was carrying his child. His only regret? Putting Patricia in a compromising position with her mother and possibly alienating himself from the woman he'd hoped to have as an ally while wooing her daughter.

"What kind of home do you think this is?" she asked. "What sort of girl do you take my daughter for? I opened my home to you, and you do not show respect for her or me."

He would have gone prostrate on the floor if he thought it would help, but nothing he could say would exonerate him from what he'd done. He found himself uttering words of apology again, which sounded so inadequate.

"I care deeply about Patricia," he added.

The corners of Aunty Ama's lips twitched, and she sighed again, a sound echoing of resignation, defeat. It cut him like a double-edged knife, because it was a direct result of his actions and reactions to situations he could have handled better.

"There are many things parents try to do for their children," she said. "Providing a better life, better opportunities, making them feel safe, keeping them healthy, and hoping they don't make the same mistakes their parents did."

Something visceral gripped him. He knew he should let it slide, count his blessings she wasn't screaming murder. He couldn't, though, because he needed to set the record straight.

"Please don't call this a mistake," he said. "It may be unplanned, it may be wrong timing, but it's not a mistake."

He'd done his best to keep his voice even in order not to rile her. Nonetheless, she stiffened, perhaps not expecting his outburst. When she didn't speak for several seconds, he expected the worst, but as she faced him, he saw none of the hatred or anger he'd expected to belie her deathly calm voice. What he saw was defeat magnified, and surprisingly the kindness she'd shown him since he arrived shone through. It stunned and tore him apart, because he didn't deserve it.

She'd welcomed him into her home, and he couldn't even manage the simple task of doing the honorable thing and keeping his hands off her daughter.

He shook the thought away, focusing on the woman sitting in front of him. Plump and short, she was so unlike his mother both in stature and character. This was someone who'd be there for her children as she'd been for her only child.

"I'm usually a good judge of character, Mr. Webber," she said. "I sensed you were a good man, that you had good intentions. Was I wrong?"

Ty was briefly thrust into memories of high school, when he'd earned himself a trip too many to the principal's office. He remembered the constant panic in his gut just before he went in, when he'd imagined the worst—dismissal. Aunty Ama's calmness scared him far more, and he knew whatever he said would ultimately determine whether he got to have Patricia in his life.

"No, ma'am," he said. "You weren't wrong."

Silence ensued. She nodded as if pondering his response. "My daughter needs a gentle hand," she said.

Ty's heart raced, hope stirred. Had she forgiven him?

"Patricia's father and I married after I got pregnant with her," she continued. "I loved him, but he wasn't sure how he felt about me, but twenty-six years ago an unwed mother was a pariah and he was a good man who did the right thing."

Ty sat back digesting the news. He'd known Patricia's father had walked away on the two most important people in his life, but he hadn't known her parents had married because of her. Finding out your parents' marriage hadn't been a love union...what a burden for a kid to carry. He knew firsthand.

It all made sense now. Why Patricia tensed up at the mention of marriage, why she didn't seem to trust he'd be there for the long haul. It was all déjà vu for her.

"We had a good enough marriage. He grew to love me, and he adored his baby girl, but there was always something missing in life for him." She cleared her throat, blinking rapidly what Ty suspected to be imminent tears. "We met in our early twenties, you see, and he had big dreams, which he gave up because of us."

Ty didn't know what to say. In any case, she didn't appear to expect a response.

"Ghana in the eighties and nineties was tough. He lost his job." She shook her head. "After months of not getting work, some friends of his came up with a scheme. They heard about work abroad, but without any property tying them to Ghana, they couldn't get visas. He met someone at the embassy who told us he could get him to America. A new identity with the required documentation."

Ty released a breath. This did not sound good. Did he want to know what happened?

"I didn't like it, but he'd begun to despair, and he saw this opportunity as his one chance for a better life for us." She looked at him, eyes misty. "He was supposed to come back for us, but after he arrived, I got two letters and that was it. I don't know if he just disappeared or if something happened to him"

"He didn't leave us?" Patricia's pained voice caused them both to start.

Ty just about died inside seeing the rawness of her grief.

"Baaba," her mother said.

"All this time I thought he'd just left us or maybe I'd done something."

"My daughter, you could never have done anything wrong."

Patricia continued as if she hadn't been interrupted. "All along you were lying to me."

Aunty Ama looked as if her daughter had backhanded her hard across the face. "Baaba, please understand—"

"No! You don't get to ask that of me. A part of me has hated him all these years for what he did." A sob escaped from her. "And when you decide to come clean, you talk to him?"

As she said the last bit, she flung a hand his way as if he was some inconsequential thing.

Wow. If he wasn't maxed out on feeling her pain, that would have finished him. He realized, though, it was her agony talking, and all he wanted was to hold her and somehow absorb her pain.

Her mother started to say something, but Patricia raised her hand to stop her. "You know what? I only came to get my bag."

With that, she turned around and re-entered the room she ran out of moments earlier. Her mother rose and started to go after her.

Ty stood, catching Aunty Ama.

"I need to talk to her," she said.

"Between you and me, I think we've put her through enough stress for one day."

She seemed to consider it for several seconds before nodding. "I always meant to tell her, you know, but the timing never seemed right."

Ty searched for a suitable response, something comforting and uplifting. Nothing came. By the rivulets streaming down her cheeks, he feared she might break down, but suddenly she straightened her posture, pulling herself together.

"You're right. She needs time and space," she said. "But she's going to need the support of her family and friends, to get past this, so I need to know if you have honorable intentions toward my daughter."

Ty hadn't let himself think about it, hadn't acknowledged it. But when he thought about it now, measured the space Patricia occupied in his heart against the only people he'd ever dared to love—his father, his sister, his aunt and his cousins—the truth stared him in the face.

"Yes," he said. "Aunty Ama, I'll be honored to have your blessing to marry her."

She made a sound Ty couldn't categorize as either a chuckle or a snort.

"If my daughter will have you, then you have my blessing."

After Aunty Ama left, Ty faced the door, which Patricia still hadn't walked out of. He suddenly found himself unsure of what to do. Go in there like he wanted to, or the more sensible thing, hang out here until she came out. He'd convinced her mother to give Patricia space, but he had a hard time taking his own advice, partly for selfish reasons—he wanted to be in the same room with her—but also because he needed to make sure she was okay.

He knocked before entering, found her seated at the study table fiddling with her phone.

"May I come in?"

"If you're looking to pick up where we left off, then no." Although she had her back to him, he heard the tears in her voice.

"It's yes then," he said, trying to lighten the mood.

He hadn't expected to get a laugh, but he'd hoped she'd turn and look at him. She didn't.

"Are you going to be okay?"

She sniffed and swiped at her cheeks with the back of her hand before turning. She hadn't answered his question, but he wouldn't hold it against her. She'd had a long and stressful day, and to be honest, all he wanted right now was to be here with her. She didn't even have to speak, although he wished she'd let him hold her, be there for her.

"I'm so angry with her right now," she said. "I can't believe she let me think he abandoned us. I mean, how is that better than telling me he went in search of greener pastures?"

"When my mother left, the certainty of knowing she'd never come back helped, because it forced me to move forward. As much as it hurt to be unwanted, I think holding on to the hope that she might have a change of heart and return would have hurt me more." He came to sit on the bed, which was the closest he could be without invading her personal space. "I'm not saying what your mother did was right, but she must have believed it to be in your best interest."

He wasn't close enough to hold her hand, but he hoped his voice carried the sentiment.

"I'm sure she did." He noted a tinge of sarcasm, but mostly, she sounded like she was trying to be a big girl about it. "It may even have been a good idea when I was little, but not after I turned eighteen." She put her phone on the table and clasped her hands on her lap. "Sometimes when I thought of him—when I missed him, I'd hate him for what he did. For lying." Regret poured into her eyes. "I should have known. I should have—"

"You were young," he said. "I'm sure deep down you still love him, and maybe that's what matters."

They fell silent. Time stretched between them, and the mood shifted. He looked past her, knowing if he let himself, he'd stare at her lips, he'd notice anew the perkiness of her breasts, the racing of her pulse from the soft flesh at the base of her neck. He sucked in a breath, reminded himself she only needed his presence. Nothing else.

She sat up suddenly. "It's late. I should probably go."

"No, stay for a little while."

He raised himself from the bed and leaned forward enough to reach her chair. She stiffened for a second, frowning until he began to drag the chair closer. She raised her legs, making it easier for him to close the space between them. When she came close enough, he abandoned the chair and took her hands.

"Dance with me."

"There's no music."

He was glad to see a spark light up in her eyes in contrast to her protest.

"Woman, you insult our heritage," he said. "Don't you know music is embedded in the African DNA?"

To his relief and delight, she gave a little laugh, allowing him to pull her into his arms. She hooked her free hand around his neck and fell into step with him.

His arms tightened a little more around her. "Now close your eyes and think of nothing."

"Except the dance."

"Not even that," he whispered.

They moved in silence for a while. Ty released a breath as the tension around his shoulders eased. For a day that had him in buoyant spirits just hours earlier, things had gone so far out of left field, he'd only now started regaining his bearings.

A tiny smile adorned Patricia's face as her arms around his neck tightened. "This is nice."

In response, he pulled her closer, moving his right hand up from the small of her back. So feminine, so supple.

His hand rose past the point where he expected her bra to interrupt the smoothness of his hand's pleasure tour. His heart lurched. *Christ*. She wasn't wearing a bra. It explained why her breasts had seemed so perky earlier. With everything going on at the time, he shouldn't have noticed, but observing things about her was a consequence of his feelings. One didn't exist without the other. She searched his eyes, cloaking him in a sensation of being exposed.

Can you read me like a book, Trish? Can you see what's in my heart?

Things he couldn't tell her because he needed to know she felt the same way about him. He shifted focus.

The last thing he wanted was for his desire to turn into an erection he couldn't do anything about. Even though his yearning to make love with her was never in question, he needed to keep his cool.

To achieve this end, he led her through a couple of turns, and as she resumed her original position in his arms, he began to hum one of his favorite R&B tunes from back in the day. Soon she was grinning, and he managed to push thoughts of sex to the background where it had to remain until they returned to Accra.

Chapter 13

A t a quarter past eleven, Patricia hoped her mother had fallen asleep. Easing the door open, she slipped in. She noticed the overhead light first. *Still on.* Her gaze immediately went to the bed where she noted, with resignation, her mother sat, reading what appeared to be a daily devotional book. So much for hoping she'd out-waited her mum.

"I don't want to talk about it," Patricia said.

Her mother didn't comment immediately. In typical Aunty Ama fashion, she remained quiet as though gathering her thoughts while Patricia changed into a nightshirt.

"One of the best pieces of advice someone gave me before marriage was never let the sun set on your anger," her mother finally said. "That's good advice for anyone and not just married couples."

Patricia wanted to point out the fact that her anger started after sunset, which technically gave her till sunset tomorrow to work through her anger but thought better of it. She could never stay angry at her mother for long.

Yet, as she faced the older woman, Patricia's heart clenched. She wanted to hold on to the justified fury, needed to let it fill her, because when she concentrated on that, she didn't have to dwell on her feelings of regret for every time she'd thought about her father in less than favorable terms, the many times she'd spoken of him with sarcasm or worse.

"Maame, you can't just quote adages and expect everything to be okay." Surprisingly, she succeeded in keeping her tone even. "You made me think he left us, and at some point, I resented him for choosing something else over us. How could you let me hate my father? A man you claim to have loved."

"I did love him," her mother said. "I *do* love him."

"Yet when you stopped hearing from him, you didn't know whether something had happened to him or he'd decided to run? Explain to me how that's love."

Her mother looked stricken. "You don't understand."

Patricia pulled up the ottoman cube by the dresser and came to sit in front of her mother. "You're the one who wanted to talk, Maame. Make me understand."

"I was warned not to let him go, that if I did, I'd never see him again."

"What?"

Just as the answer occurred, her mother continued.

"Menaesi—"

"Don't tell me this is all due to something Menaesi predicted!"

"Here me out, Baaba," her mother said.

Patricia clamped her lips together, despite her instinct to end the conversation immediately.

"She told me if I let him go, I'd be setting him free. I didn't want to let him go, but I had to believe he would come back if we were meant to be."

"When will you stop listening to the old woman?

What does 'setting him free' even mean?"

"I've never begrudged you for not believing in Menaesi's third eye, so don't belittle my choice to believe." Her mother's indignant tone stopped Patricia from giving a retort. "Your father gave up his dreams of furthering his studies and becoming an engineer. Instead, he found work to earn money for our upkeep. Without us holding him back, he could be free to do this, and the possibilities abroad were endless."

Patricia sat back, staring at her mother. For the first time, she saw the older woman not as her mother, but as the insecure young girl she must have been when she said goodbye to her husband. "You didn't have faith in your love for each other?" she said.

"I had you to take care of, and I couldn't afford to miss him when you needed me, so I told myself he had seen the separation as an escape. You kept asking about your father, and you would cry for him every time I tried to discipline you, and so I made you believe he left us."

Patricia remembered some of it. All those times she'd lose a tooth and pray on it for her father to return, times she'd hid in her room and cried because someone had called her a bastard—an undesirable.

Her mother's hands closed around her balled fists on her lap, and she finally looked Patricia in the eye. "I was wrong to keep the truth from you, Baaba."

Patricia couldn't bring herself to speak. Her mind had shifted to overdrive, trying to make a modicum of sense out of the information overload. Over twenty years of keeping all this to herself, her mother decided to dump it all in one night, a night on which Patricia was already on an emotional rollercoaster.

"Forgive your mother, *medie*."

Mine. An endearment her mother used to favor during Patricia's childhood. It softened the edges of Patricia's anger, but didn't do anything about the sorrow.

"We need to go to bed, Maame."

Her mother's eyes widened slightly as if she hadn't expected those words, but she accepted it and released Patricia's hands. "Okay, my daughter."

Patricia exhaled, relieved her mother hadn't tried to push her. *Maame* had been her strength growing up, and despite emotional scars sustained through their journeys of life and survival, they'd both turned out okay. Eventually, she'd have to stop being angry at her mum, but at this moment she couldn't bring herself to utter the words.

ભ૦ભ૦

The next morning, Patricia was ready to hit the road by seven o'clock. Contrary to her expectations, her mother hadn't tried to continue their conversation from last night. Instead, while Patricia took her shower and packed her things, her mother insisted on preparing breakfast. Even though Patricia couldn't wait to return to Accra where she could get some alone time to think, skipping meals was a luxury she couldn't afford.

So far, she'd been lucky. Her nausea stuck to morning hours soon after she woke up. Two or three oranges with every meal took care of the unsavory sensation in the mouth that caused spitting.

Soon after breakfast, they bid goodbye to her family and set off for Accra.

She couldn't help drawing comparisons with their journey four days before. While the other had been filled with lively discourse, a stark lack of conversation characterized this one. She didn't attempt to fill it, though. She had enough going on in her head without having to force small talk. Foremost in her mind was what to do about Ty. One moment, he was making love with her, gradually coaxing her heart into the equation, then the next instant he became someone she didn't recognize at all.

Any other man, she'd already have banished from her life. She held firmly to the belief that some people came into one's life for just a moment, and if anyone's presence caused her more stress than necessary, she had no problem weeding them out. Consequently, she had only a handful of trusted friends. The question was why hadn't she kicked Ty to the curb? He'd become more stressful to have around.

She kept her gaze on the passing scenes outside, a lineup of tables displaying Fante *kenkey*, a dumpling made from fermented corn dough wrapped in plantain leaves and steamed—her landmark for the village of Ya-moransa, and also one of the first signs signaling they'd truly left Cape Coast behind. She breathed relief with each passing second they drove farther away.

Normally, she'd be filled with a tinge of sadness and wishing for more time in the serene, laidback city, but this time her stay had been like a journey to the twilight zone and she'd sooner forget it.

Except, so many things about this trip made it more memorable than any of her previous visits—touring the city with Ty, experiencing the castle with him, seeing it through his eyes, their lovemaking, which she probably shouldn't think about if she wanted to stop the spiraling of her heart.

A smiled tugged at her lips as she remembered their dance last night. She'd half expected it to be a ploy to butter her up before blindsiding her with something else. He'd however surprised her by being the old Ty, the man she'd met nearly four months ago—not the one who threatened her with an all but forgotten tradition with a look in his eyes that had her worrying about what he was capable of.

He'd certainly looked like he'd do it if she dared him. She'd been smart enough not to call his bluff. Once they reached Accra, she needed to regain control, re-establish the ground rules, and show Ty he couldn't bully her into submission.

At least it had been the plan until the dance. He'd reminded her of the first time they'd met, how they'd instantly gelled even before discovering the things they had in common. It had been fun—and she'd needed that. She'd hoped to have danced long enough for her mother to be asleep by the time Patricia retired to bed, but the woman was resilient.

She didn't want to think about the dance or the conversation her mother had started.

She looked at Ty as he hummed to the R&B classics on the radio, intermittently singing along. For a guy with the boring title of financial consultant, he was funky and knew how to get his groove on, as the Americans would say. Among the many non-typical things about him, the stud in his left earlobe—which, wonder of all wonders, her mother hadn't commented on—and a ring on his little finger. Then again, it suited him.

As if he sensed her watching, he turned. She looked away, her face heating up, then feeling silly for her reaction, she turned back.

"Admiring my kingly head again?"

She chuckled. "Don't let it get to your head."

He laughed at the pun.

"I'm thinking about the dance last night," she said. "I enjoyed it."

"You did?" he teased. "I couldn't tell from all the smiling and giggling."

"What can I say? I keep my emotions close to my heart."

Eish! She'd meant it as a joke, but it didn't come out

right, and she knew why. She'd spoken the truth—she didn't let people get too close. Most people blamed it on what her father had done, thinking she feared if she let anyone in, they'd leave her too. In all fairness, this was the truth—the original truth.

She kept relationships physical, because sex was easy. It was intense and pleasurable, and lasted for only moments. Then you got back to your life. After living like this for so long, she'd perfected it. Sometimes she wondered if *she* had become the problem, the one who couldn't commit.

Ty's gaze paused on her a couple of seconds longer than necessarily safe for driving at a hundred kilometers per hour before he faced forward. If he could feel her stare, he didn't show it. She continued to study his profile, long enough for the forbidden, crazy thought to enter her mind.

What if she said yes?

For a few seconds she pictured it—coming home each day to Ty's welcoming kiss, his strong presence a permanent fixture in her life, making love with him every night for the rest of their lives, making more babies—

The ever-present voice of reason sliced through her thoughts, dishing out its daily dose of reality. She may have broken their deal and begun falling for him, but the feelings weren't reciprocated.

Even if they were, their lives were literally thousands of miles apart, and it would be cruel to her child to give her a here-today-there-tomorrow dad.

She took in a deep breath, exhaled through her mouth. The silence continued for the rest of the journey, punctuated with the barest of conversations, mostly of Ty asking questions about sights and sounds they drove past and she providing the relevant details.

Due to heavy traffic when entering Accra, it took

them more than two hours to get from the outskirts to Patricia's place.

"Home sweet home," she said, looking up at the apartment.

She'd meant the expression as a triviality, something said for want of something to say, but the little tug in her heart indicated otherwise. She *had* missed home—her space and sanctuary. She turned to him. Would he expect her to invite him up? How did she tell him she wanted to be alone today without starting an argument or hurting his feelings?

As if he'd read her mind, he said, "I can't come up."

"That's okay. I have things to do, anyway." She didn't try to feign disappointment lest he change his mind. "What are you doing the rest of the day?"

Baaba Patricia, what are you doing? Why ask about his plans when she needed to withdraw from him? At least until her emotions were in check.

"I'm moving house."

She raised her brows. "Oh?"

"I forgot to mention it. Thane has been helping me find a long-stay apartment. I couldn't reside at a hotel the entire time I'm here. Plus, staying at a hotel makes me feel like a stranger in town."

The tiniest twinge punched her in the gut. This was the first she'd heard about him moving, and she shouldn't care. After all, he had no obligation to share such information with her. They'd only seen each other *every* day for at least four days running, during which time *he* had become privy to several intimate details of her life, and he *forgot to mention*?

He frowned. "Did I say something wrong?"

"No," she replied. *You said nothing.* Pasting on a smile, she added, "Happy moving."

She yanked the handle and released the door.

"Hey." He touched her arm making her turn. "Can I call you tonight?"

She should have said no and established the new rules—share nothing personal, spend only as much time together as required, and absolutely no nightly phone calls. If they had sex, and that was a big if, there would be no pillow talk, no cuddling, and no breakfast in the morning.

He smiled, turning her brain to mush, and she heard herself saying, "Okay."

Shamed at her own lack of conviction, she slid out, opened the back door, and took out her valise. She had enough presence of mind to shut the door without slamming it.

As he drove off, he blew her a kiss and her heart fluttered. She waved him goodbye and watched him drive off until the car disappeared around the corner. Then she stood several moments longer, berating herself for doing what had to be the most wifely thing ever.

෨෧෨

When Patricia entered her apartment, she locked the door and walked straight to the bedroom. Placing the valise on the floor next to the door, she didn't bother drawing the curtains to let in the afternoon sunlight. She preferred the muted tones from the little sunlight managing to filter through the layered voile curtains. She lowered herself onto the bed, kicking off her slip-on shoes, and stretched out on her back. She placed her palms over her lower abdomen and released the breath she felt like she'd been holding since yesterday.

Her hand caressed her stomach, for even though the baby hadn't started kicking yet, knowing he or she was there gave her a wholeness of being which seemed to alleviate the occasional loneliness of having no one in her life. It was the same kind of completeness Ty gave her, the kind she dared not hold on to.

In her moment of relaxation, she'd let her guard down and emotions she'd held at bay for the past couple of days came crashing in. Mostly of her father.

Pushing aside the thoughts, she turned to her side. She pulled the extra pillow and cuddled it. Even though she hadn't given her mother the satisfaction of her forgiveness, she couldn't stay angry forever. However misguided her reasons, Patricia believed her mother's intentions had been pure.

She supposed there existed a remote possibility that her father had indeed seen his trip as an escape. If so, had he forgotten about them and made a new family somewhere along the line? If not, then only one possibility remained. Something had happened to him. Was he even alive? Was she ready to deal with the answer?

Maybe she was no different from her mother.

She blinked, releasing the build-up of tears in her eyes. For the first time ever, being like her mother didn't fill her with pride. Her chin began to tremble as control on her emotions slipped and deep wrenching sobs took over. After years of resenting her dad and locking out thoughts of him, she finally let herself miss him.

He'd have known what to do about Patricia's current situation. At the very least he'd have provided a man's perspective and maybe even the right strategy to convince Ty to let go. If he'd been around, she might not even be in this soup in the first place. Not that her mother hadn't been a good mum, but fathers were legendary for being overprotective when it came to their daughters.

Even though her mother had given her "the talk" the very day of Patricia's first menstrual period, Maame had never been one of those parents who preached virginity until marriage. Even so, her many nuggets of wisdom ensured Patricia hadn't started exploring her sexuality until after she turned seventeen.

No doubt the presence of a father would have delayed her first experience even further. If she'd been a virgin when she'd met Ty, the sheer maleness of him would have had her running the other way instead of being drawn to him like a moth to a flame. How much simpler things would have been then. No baby, no proposal, no possibility of falling for Ty.

She'd certainly not be lying here thinking about last night when they'd parted ways, how he'd brushed his lips against hers in a gesture so brief and so by-the-way it had felt like second nature, like something he did every night.

She released a sigh and forced her eyes shut, praying for sleep to claim her just so she didn't spend the rest of the afternoon staring at the clock and anticipating the call he'd promised her.

That would be pathetic.

Chapter 14

The whole way back to the hotel, Ty had to talk himself out of turning around and going back to Patricia's. It must have been the look in her eyes when he'd told her about moving, or maybe the way she'd stood at the roadside watching him until he turned the corner. The only reason he kept driving was the instinct cautioning him to give her space. After invading her life the past few days, he had to give her that much, even though every selfish instinct in him wanted to do otherwise.

Within an hour of reaching the hotel, he'd packed and completed check-out formalities. Thane arrived just in time to lead him to the new apartment. Ty followed in the rental, which he'd decided to keep for another few days. Twenty minutes later, they were passing through a residential neighborhood with a lot of gated properties hidden behind high walls. It looked upper class, neat and peaceful, though Ty couldn't help thinking it must be lonely here too.

He preferred neighborhoods where people interacted freely with their neighbors. Even in the US, he didn't spend much time in the high-rise apartment he kept in Manhattan for when business took him to the Big Apple. He preferred his less ritzy place in New Rochelle, which couldn't boast of the kind of view the Manhattan skyline provided, but where he had a few friendly neighbors.

Leaving the neighborhood behind, they drove past a school and through an area where the walls rose no more than waist high. Children could be seen playing in some compounds, and a few kiosks selling pre-paid cell phone credit graced the roadsides. Thane signaled and slowed to a stop in front of one of a cluster of six houses. While each property had its own compound, the short walls and picketed gates ensured privacy while providing a good view of the surroundings. Ty instantly liked it.

He exited his car and looked around, noticing a sign board with an address identifying the locality.

"La-bone," he read.

Thane chuckled. "The 'e' isn't silent."

"Labon-e," Ty said, and since his friend didn't say anything further, he assumed he'd gotten it right this time.

"We had a service clean up the place yesterday, so you're good to go," Thane said when they entered.

"Thanks, man."

"I'd stay for a beer, but I have to meet Naaki in thirty minutes."

Ty hadn't expected his friend to stay, but he also figured that wasn't the point of the remark. "There's beer?"

"You have Naaki to thank for that and your stocked fridge."

Ty smiled. Naaki was sweet and thoughtful, and perfect for Thane, just as he and Patricia were perfect together, even if she wouldn't admit it.

"Tell her I said thank you. I know you'd have left me high and dry."

"Hey, you're the best man," Thane said. "You work for me."

Ty chuckled, shaking his head. "Didn't you have somewhere to be?"

Laughing, Thane handed over the keys, before heading out.

Finally alone, Ty familiarized himself with the furnished two-bedroom bungalow. The two bedrooms and their shared bathroom, the kitchenette and living area doubling as a dining room were all to his liking. After taking his suitcase to one bedroom, he went to the fridge and got a beer before settling down in the living room.

He checked his watch. Was it too early to call Patricia? The urge to head back to her place assaulted him once again, and he found himself setting down the bottle and wavering in his resolve to give her space. He shouldn't miss her, since they'd said goodbye barely five hours ago.

During the three months they'd been apart, he'd thought about her a lot, often replaying memories of her in his mind. He supposed that amounted to missing her, but this felt different. She'd become a constant fixture in his mind, and each moment spent in her presence heightened his desire to spend even more time with her. Not only did he find himself replaying their conversations and activities in his mind, he caught himself creating new scenarios he'd like to enact with her.

Wasn't that what a person did when he met someone he wanted to make a part of his life forever?

"Crazy," he muttered.

For a guy who hadn't planned for marriage and family until some ten years down the line, he should have been in a mad panic, but impending fatherhood and his feelings for Patricia brought on a surprising sense of calm.

He set down the beer and sat back, letting his mind drift to the last time they'd made love. She'd branded him until he didn't want to know who he was without her, and then she'd thrown it all back in his face. After everything he'd discovered about her past, he understood why she'd want to push him away.

He knew all about the sense of cautiousness people developed after being hurt by loved ones and even life itself. Before her, he'd been the same, not letting anyone close enough to care about them, ending relationships before they got complicated, believing the people you loved the most were the ones who could hurt you the worst.

The problem with people like him and Patricia was, they hid all their baggage under a cloak of practicality, which was hard to dispute.

His phone rang, the shrill sound piercing through his thoughts and jolting him out of his imaginings. The screen identified the caller as Patricia.

He tried not to sound too eager when he answered, "Hi."

For several seconds, he could only hear her breathing, then, "I know you said you'd call later, but—"

"I'm glad you called."

Another moment of silence passed. "How's your new place?"

"Quiet," he said truthfully. *Lonely.*

Normally, he didn't mind his own company, but after four days in Cape Coast with her and her family, the aloneness hit him hard.

"I guess I should let you settle in."

"I have one suitcase, a backpack, and a laptop. There isn't much to settling in."

She made a sound like a chuckle, which brought a smile to his lips. Her effect on him, more potent than any other woman had managed, grew each passing day. The sound of her voice alone filled him with a sense of peace, her embrace a feeling of belonging. When she looked at him, her eyes told him he wasn't just another guy in her life, but she wouldn't let herself consider their connection beyond great sex and the fact of the child they were having.

He had to show her she needed him as much as he needed her. But how?

Truth be told, after their mostly silent drive back to Accra, he'd half expected her to withdraw, making it harder for him to woo her, which made this call so unexpected.

"Why did you call?" To his ears, he hadn't sounded harsh, but the silence following his question made him wonder how else he could have put it. "I mean, is everything okay?"

She sighed. "I don't know. I guess my house is a little quiet, too."

Her answer hung between them, taunting him.

Do you want to come over? The words made it to the tip of his tongue before he reined them in, reminding himself she needed space even if the signal she seemed to be sending said otherwise. Any other day, any other woman, he might have asked her over and shown her enough of a good time to make her temporarily forget her woes.

However, he cared about Patricia too much to do that, so instead of what was really on his mind, he said, "We must both be missing your mom's house and cooking."

She chuckled. "Yeah."

Seconds of silence ticked by.

"Have you called her?" he asked.

"Not yet. I will call shortly to let her know we've arrived safely."

"You need to forgive her."

"I know."

"She needs to hear it."

"I know."

"You should tell her today, even if you don't feel like it right now."

"No wonder she took to you so quickly."

He smiled. The disappointment in her voice nearly made him change his mind about asking her over. Luckily, she took that option off the table.

"See you tomorrow?"

"Yeah," he replied.

After she hung up, he put the phone down and stared at the half empty bottle of beer. God, if Thane could have witnessed that conversation, he'd laugh Ty out of the room. Giving a snort of laughter, he took a sip of the drink, then grimaced because it was no longer as cold as he liked it.

୧৩୧

Patricia woke up early on Sunday morning still feeling like a complete idiot. What had she been thinking calling Ty yesterday when he'd promised to call her? What a desperate, un-Patricia-like move. She'd stopped short of inviting herself over. Thankfully, he hadn't extended an invitation either. If he had, she wouldn't have said no. So much for resetting the ground rules.

After the restless night she'd had, she needed an intervention in the form of her best friend. She couldn't wait to for their usual breakfast meeting. A conversation with Naaki would help her sort out her muddled feelings and thoughts. Since they hadn't spoken last night, and she didn't want to risk Naaki making other plans, she reached for her phone from the bedside unit. Checking the time and realizing it was only six-thirty, she opted to send a text.

Breakfast?

The reply came back fifteen minutes later. *Of course!*

Patricia smiled, knowing her friend would want details on her trip with Ty to Cape Coast. Naaki had no idea how much there was to tell.

Patricia arrived at the Infusions Café at eight. Naaki had sent a text that she was five minutes away, so Patricia ordered two cups of tea. The order arrived just as Naaki's VW beetle came to a halt in front of the café. By the time she joined Patricia at the table, the waitress had finished pouring their beverages.

"Would you like to order anything else?"

"You must be new," Naaki remarked. "Is Ewurama off today?"

The waitress replied in the affirmative, adding an apology.

"No worries," Patricia said, and they proceeded to order an Infusion breakfast special, a modified full English breakfast, consisting of two sausages, two eggs, two pancakes, two slices of toasted bread, fried mushrooms and a serving of *kelewele*—fried pieces of ripe plantain seasoned with local spices. Served with a large pot of coffee or tea, it was such a big meal that one order was usually enough for two.

As soon as the waitress left their table, Naaki turned to her. "Okay, spill."

Patricia grinned. "What makes you think there's anything to spill?"

"First of all, you went to Cape Coast *with Ty*. As if that's not reason enough, you sent me a text once about your safe arrival, and I didn't hear from you until your SOS this morning."

"It wasn't an SOS."

Naaki raised an eyebrow. "Please, normally, you'd call me when you were stepping out of the house and ask, 'are you on your way?' without greeting, I might add."

"Okay you got me." She sighed. "Cape Coast was a disaster."

Naaki's expression immediately turned to concern. "Is your mum okay? Is it Menaesi?"

"Oh, believe me they're both fine. Mum got a clean bill of health, and while we were at the hospital, my traitorous great aunt decided to educate Ty about our marriage customs."

"I don't see the disaster part."

"Menaesi told Ty he could marry me without my consent."

"Wow."

"Exactly."

"How did that happen? Weren't you supposed to not take him home?"

"Let's just say fate had other plans." She stirred her tea. "Did you bring the honey?"

Naaki nodded, retrieving the six-ounce bottle of honey she often carried in her handbag. Patricia took it and squeezed a teaspoon into her mug. She handed over the honey to Naaki who took it but continued to look at her expectantly instead of sweetening her tea. Patricia recounted how Ty had ended up meeting her mother and grandaunt, and her mother finding out about the baby.

"Needless to say, Menaesi already *knew*." She made air quotes at "knew."

"Maybe it's the same way she knows Ty is going to make you happy," Naaki teased.

"Oh, please." Patricia rolled her eyes. "She's just a

cunning old woman. I'm sure, at eighty-four, she's picked up more than a few tricks."

Naaki chuckled, sipping her tea. "Seriously, would it be such a bad thing to end up with Ty?"

Patricia considered it for a second, remembering the moment of insanity when she'd actually flirted with the idea of saying yes.

"I don't know," she admitted. "I certainly don't want to end up with the kind of guy who'd even consider a forced marriage."

"What makes you think Ty is that kind of guy?"

"Let's see. The fact that he actually said he would."

Naaki laughed, earning herself a glare from Patricia.

"I'm glad you're taking this seriously."

Though Naaki had stopped laughing, her eyes remained elated. "Come on, I'll bet he only said it to get a reaction out of you."

'*You have no idea what I'd do for my kid.*' The words echoed in her head, a stark reminder she couldn't afford to make any assumptions about Ty.

"He got a reaction all right."

She really didn't want to dwell on that conversation.

Thankfully, her friend didn't probe. Instead, she said, "Your mum must be thrilled about the baby, though."

Patricia frowned. "Strangely, she seemed rather cool and collected. She didn't even give Ty the third degree for getting her little girl pregnant. Instead, she got all emotional and told him about my father."

Naaki paused in the process of reaching for her mug, brows creased. "Really?"

"That's the other thing," Patricia replied. "He may not have set out to abandon us."

This time, her friend gaped at her. "What?"

Patricia related everything she'd learned about her father. When she finished, there was silence at the table.

Naaki reached forward and squeezed her hand. "How are you feeling about all this?"

"Confused. Angry. Sad. Take your pick." Patricia sighed. "I mean, objectively, I know he probably *did* walk out on us, because if he didn't, shouldn't he have returned by now?" She paused, although she didn't expect an answer. "I'm so pissed. I'd made my peace with it, you know. Now I'm back to thinking maybe he's out there somewhere. It's like I'm six-years-old again and waiting for my father to come home." She had to pause again, this time to regain her composure. "What if he's not out there somewhere?"

The significance of the question left them both without words. With her free hand, Patricia took a long sip of her tea, not tasting the liquid as it paved a warm path to her stomach.

Before either of them could say anything more, the waitress brought their breakfast along with a fresh pot of tea.

"Would you like anything else?" she asked,

They both shook their heads and the waitress left.

Patricia looked at her friend. Normally, Naaki knew exactly what to say to make her believe things weren't as bad as they seemed. This time, her friend seemed at a loss. Since Patricia didn't herself know what to say, she picked up her cutlery and dished some of the food on to her plate. Naaki followed suit.

They ate mostly in silence, and the little conversation they had pertained to the wedding. When they had finished eating, the waitress came to clear the table.

"Look, Pat," Naaki finally said. "I have no idea what to say about your dad. Maybe he's somewhere out there and maybe you'll find him someday, but what I do know is that, even though he's not around, he's still running your life."

"What are you talking about?"

"You've made so many decisions and you have all these rules you live by based on what he did or didn't do."

"Well, if you put it that way…"

"Take it from someone who had to let go of her rules to find love," Naaki added with a little smile.

Patricia smiled too. "I should have known you'd somehow work Thane into this conversation."

"It wasn't intentional, I promise," Naaki said with a giggle. "I'm serious, though. You should let loose. Have a yes day."

"A yes day?"

"A day in which you don't over-think anything, especially about all the reasons you shouldn't do something you really want to do. When someone asks you to do something, you say…"

Naaki left the sentence hanging, cueing Patricia to finish it off.

"Let me guess. Yes."

"Ding, ding, ding, ding."

Patricia shook her head. "Where did you come up with that one?"

"Thane." She laughed. "Hey, you asked. The rules are, you can't hurt anyone, including yourself, and you shouldn't do anything permanent."

Patricia was certain "permanent" meant something like a tattoo, but Patricia's mind went straight to Ty's proposal. *Make that* persistent *proposals*.

She snapped out of her thoughts as Naaki took a hold of both Patricia's hands. "I think for you a day isn't enough. You should make it a yes week."

Patricia shook her head. "It's a ridiculous idea."

Yet it had sunk in, making her question her own words. Maybe her friend had a point. Maybe she needed to not over-think things. She shook herself mentally. *I can't really be considering this.*

"What do you say?" Naaki persisted. "It could be fun."

She took in a deep breath. "I guess."

"Wrong answer."

With a chuckle, she amended her response. "Yes."

Chapter 15

Several hours after breakfast, as Patricia mulled over her conversation with Naaki, she decided the "yes" thing could do her some good, especially given the condition of not getting into any permanent situations. She'd run different scenarios in her mind and none seemed scary or damaging. She even conceded to needing an attitude adjustment—even if only for a week. If nothing at all, *it could be fun.*

Still in high spirits, she decided to put her elation to good use by working on Beauty by Patricia. She hadn't touched it in several days and it was more than due for some attention. She set up at her dining table instead of going downstairs as she normally would, and within two and a half hours, she had a first real draft of her business plan—enough for a lengthy discussion with Ty the next time they sat together on it.

And just like that, her mind shifted gears from work to Ty. He hadn't called yet, but she'd resolved to avoid a repetition of yesterday. After all, they'd promised to see each other today so he'd have to call at some point. If she wanted him to know she was serious about them going their separate ways, then she needed to stop exhibiting behavior he could interpret as mixed signals.

However, her gaze kept drifting over to the phone every few seconds. *Get a grip, girl.* When admonishing herself didn't seem to work, she realized she had to physically distance herself from the phone before her desire to hear Ty's voice won over her decision to play it cool. She picked up her laptop and moved to the couch where the phone would no longer be in her line of vision.

It worked for thirty minutes, during which time she wrapped up, answered some emails, and posted updates on her social media platforms. As she shut down, the sound of her phone ringing caused her to start. She stood, eagerness propelling her forward, making her rush to grab the phone as if fearing it would stop ringing.

Pushing the answer button, she paused for a couple of seconds to take in a deep, steadying breath. "Hello?"

"Hi."

She took in another breath to calm her racing heart.

"Were you running?"

"Kind of. I'd left the phone on the dining table while doing some work on the couch," she explained, although she knew the sound of his voice probably had more to do with it, considering the short distance she'd covered to get to the phone.

"It's called a mobile phone for a reason."

"I know, but I was trying very hard not to call you." *Crap.* Why on earth had she told him the truth?

"Oh?"

"Don't take it the wrong way. I just didn't want t—"

"Uh-huh?"

He sounded more amused than anything else and suddenly, she found herself laughing.

"Can we start over?"

"Depends. Do I still get to see you today?"

"Yes."

"Great. What would you like us to do?"

She sank onto the nearest chair. "Your wish is my command," she answered with a chuckle. *Naaki's going to love this.*

"How about I pick you up and take you to my place?" Ty suggested. "We can make dinner and spend the evening in."

"That's what you want to do?"

"Too boring?"

"Not at all. I actually don't want to go out, so an evening in sounds perfect."

"In that case, how about I up the ante?"

She frowned. "I'm afraid to ask."

"Don't be so suspicious," he said. "Pack a bag. Stay the night."

It took a moment for her to respond. "Are you serious?"

She didn't do overnight stays at guys' places. It screamed commitment, created expectations she didn't want hanging over her head. Especially where Ty was concerned.

"Come on, Trish. We've already spent the night together before, and we're having a baby. Doesn't that make me an exception to the rule?"

She wanted to remind him the last time he'd spent the night at her place, he'd proposed marriage the morning after, but Naaki's words echoed in her mind, and she bit back the words. If she was going to do the yes week, then she might as well jump in with both feet. After all, if he proposed again, all she had to do was say no.

"I don't know about that, but I promised Naaki I'd venture outside my comfort zone for a change."

"Oh, really? How far out of your comfort zone are we talking?"

That earned him a laugh. "I guess you'll just have to wait and find out."

They spoke a few more minutes, and after agreeing to a meeting time, they ended the conversation.

Within an hour, Patricia had showered, picked an outfit, discarded it for another, and packed the overnight bag. She couldn't believe she'd let Ty talk her into sleeping over. She'd expected to suddenly grow cold feet, but funny enough, she found herself thinking up ways of making the most of the night.

"First time for everything," she muttered.

She paused in thought. It seemed each time she and Ty had spent a full night together, something significant happened. *Coincidence or fate?* She shook her head. No thinking or rationalizing, she reminded herself. As long as she didn't wake up married, she'd survive whatever craziness tomorrow morning brought.

୧୬୧୬

Ty had planned an innocent evening with Patricia. For once, he would spend the night with her without making love. Tough as that would be, because he *always* wanted to make love with her, he'd realized the only way to convince her to be his wife was to prove to her—and maybe a little bit to himself—they had more in common than great sex. He needed to show her they could be like any other couple out there who came home from work, had dinner, cuddled in front of the TV, and then went to bed.

Tonight, he planned on making beef stroganoff to go with noodles, topped off with coconut crème brûlée for dessert. Nothing said home and family better than a good meal and a creamy dessert. Besides, he figured if he stuffed himself enough, he'd stand a better chance of not changing his mind, because *that* wasn't an option. He couldn't expect her to change her mind if *he* wasn't ready to make some sacrifices. A few nights without sex in exchange for a lifetime together was a trade he'd gladly make.

When he arrived at her place shortly after five o'clock, he couldn't help noticing a group of kids playing soccer in front of a house up ahead. A smile crept to his lips bringing with it thoughts of playing ball with his child someday. He chuckled. What was it about watching other people's children that made you love yours even more?

With a general happy disposition bubbling inside, he made his way up the stairs and rapped at Patricia's front door.

"It's open," she called from inside.

Ty entered and secured the door. "Trish?"

The chink of cutlery told him she was in the kitchen, from where she called out, "I'll be out in a minute. Please, have a seat."

Like a good future husband, he went to sit. He didn't turn on the TV, opting rather to mentally go over the dos-and-don'ts for tonight. In the past, spending the night with a woman definitely involved sex. Otherwise, he preferred to sleep alone. The fact that he wanted this, had *planned* it, meant—

"All set," Patricia's voice cut short his thoughts.

He looked up, pausing as their gazes locked. She had a sparkle in her eyes—something he'd seen a lot of when they'd first met, but this had to be the first time she seemed excited to see him on this trip. Did it mean anything?

"You look beautiful," he said, drinking in the sight of

her, breathtaking in a flirty lace blouse and a figure flat-tering skirt, which showed off her new curves and cute knees.

His mind started from there, imagining sliding the skirt farther up to expose her thighs, his hands feathering her silken skin, slipping underneath the skirt to steal an intimate caress; her voice in his ears, egging him on; her body wrapped around him, surrounding him. He could have sworn he heard a moan, then he realized it had come from him.

He swore silently and shoved the images out of his mind, focusing rather on what she held in her hand.

"My favorite South African wine," she declared. "I don't know what's for dinner, but I hope this goes with it."

Concern knitted through his brows. "Aren't you sup-posed to avoid alcohol?"

"The wine is for you," she answered, raising her oth-er hand. "I'm drinking juice."

She put both in a bag, which she placed on the dining table.

"Dinner is a surprise." He stood, walked over to her, and picked up the drinks. "I can tell you, though, a Cab-ernet-Sauvignon will go very nicely with it, but if you're having juice, so will I."

"You don't have to."

"Remember the last time I drank, and you didn't?"

Her answering smile held a radiance that made him want to reach for her and kiss her senseless.

"Fair enough," she said. "You can drink your wine when I'm not around."

"Shall we?" he said.

"What's the hurry?" She took the bag from his grasp and placed it back on the table, then closed the space be-tween them. "I think we have time for—" She did a little finger-walk on his chest, "—a little something."

Oh, boy. Right there laid the flaw in his plan.

Her lips brushed his, then she pulled back leaving just a breath between them. She tilted her head slightly, looking into his eyes—an invitation proffered, and he found himself caught in a catch twenty-two. If he stopped her now, he could ruin the night for her, but if he didn't, then he stood the risk of ruining his plan.

However, with Patricia's breasts pressing lightly on his chest and her scent exerting a pheromonal effect on him, he did what any sane man would do. With one hand, he cupped the back of her head and brought her lips back to his. She led, deftly parting his lips with her warm tongue. Of its own volition, his other hand settled on her bottom, nudged her forward until she was plastered against him. He grunted as she shimmied against his hardness, and she moaned in response. She pulled her hip back just enough for her hand to slide between them and find his member. It was like a jolt of electricity passing through his veins, jerking him out of the luscious sensations swirling within him.

"If we don't leave now, we might run into heavy traffic," he said, his voice holding zero conviction.

She gave him a coy smile. "I don't mind a little traffic."

He groaned again. As much as he liked her capitulation from previous days, he loved when she took charge.

Her fingers skillfully unbuckled his belt and worked down his fly. She yanked the jeans down his hip and then closed her hand around his hard length. Even with his boxers between them, her touch seared. As she rubbed him, her lips moved from his mouth to his chin, then his neck, his chest…

By the time she got to her knees in front of him, his pants had dropped down to his ankles, and his boxers were around his hips, his erection at nearly ninety degrees. With her lips hovering inches away, her warm breath fanning his manhood, she raised her head. The sight of her looking at him through her lashes intensified the anticipation.

"Still worried about traffic?"

Was she kidding? He wasn't even thinking about his plan to have a platonic night. Well, technically this wasn't sex.

She passed her tongue over his tip, and even that rationalization flew out the window.

"To hell with traffic," he rasped.

Smiling, she licked him again, causing his manhood to jerk. A ripple of shivers ran down his being. His pelvic muscles clenched. If she didn't take him in right now, he was going to have to take matters into his own hands.

Her tongue swirled around his tip before her mouth closed in on him. He shuddered. A guttural sound emanated from him that wasn't quite a groan. "Ah, honey."

She responded with a soft moan. His hands moved to cradle her head, and he closed his eyes as his mind emptied of everything except Patricia and the sensations consuming him.

ഇരുഇ

"I think I left my brain in your house," Ty said when they finally hit the road.

He couldn't erase the image of Patricia on her knees, taking him into her mouth the way she had.

The sound of her laughter surrounded them, filled him, making him question his decision to avoid further intimacy tonight.

"The night is still young," she said.

Ty realized how this evening could go, how quickly

his endgame would shift to the backburner if he didn't take his mind off the promise in her voice.

"My mum sends her regards, by the way," she said.

Ty exhaled relief. If he kept the conversation on general topics, his endgame wouldn't wander too far from his mind. He grasped it with both hands. "My regards back to her."

"Thanks for the advice to tell her I forgive her. I think we both needed to hear it."

Ty smiled. "Glad to help."

"She wanted to know if your name stands for Tyler, like Tyler Perry, and I realized I had no idea."

Ty laughed. "She knows about Tyler Perry?"

"She's been watching *If Loving You Is Wrong* on TV."

"I'm just Ty," he said. "My dad wanted to name me Tyler after himself, and my mother preferred Tyson. They couldn't agree."

"If they were Ghanaian, your dad would have won," she said. "In all tribes I know of, the father names the children."

He raised his brows. "What happened to matrilineal inheritance?"

"The kids belong to the woman, but the man officially names them," she answered.

As conversations went, this had to be as mundane as they came, but it seemed to strengthen his connection to her.

"Have you thought of a name for our baby yet?"

When she didn't answer immediately, he glanced her way. She looked at him with a curious smile.

"What?" he asked, returning his attention to the road.

"I expected you to latch on to 'the man officially names them.'"

He reached out his right hand and placed it on her

lap, caressing lightly. "You're carrying the baby for nine months. I think you should get a bigger say in choosing a name."

Her hand covered his, squeezing tightly for a few seconds before letting go. "Nyamekye, meaning God's gift," she said. "It's my mother's middle name, but it's unisex."

"It's a good name." He attempted to repeat it. "*Nya-me-che.*"

She giggled. "Not bad. You can add an English name."

He thought about it a bit. "Tyler, after my dad, if it's a boy."

"If it's a girl?"

"Tyrene."

Chapter 16

Patricia wasn't an idiot. She knew a life with Ty wouldn't constitute of days like today, in which a series of ordinary events culminated into a perfect whole.

From her apartment, they hadn't encountered much of the traffic Ty had feared. Arriving at his place shortly before seven o'clock, Ty had taken her valise to the bedroom. He'd poured them each a glass of grape juice, sticking to his promise of not taking alcohol if she couldn't. Speaking of dinner, she didn't think she'd seen anything sexier than watching him don an apron and whip up an elaborate meal, including an oh-so-delicious crème brûlée. She'd known he cooked, of course, but she hadn't realized the extent of his cooking prowess.

He'd allowed her to help only with setting the table where they'd eaten in the ambiance of demure sconce lighting. It came as no surprise to discover Ty was a great conversationalist when he wasn't being a great lover. They'd taken dessert to the couch where a bit of the custard allegedly at the corners of her lips had led to toe-curling, heavy-duty making out.

Now she lay wrapped in his arms, basking in the sensation of his skin against hers as his fingers caressed her hair. Their conversation in the car had remained with her. Picking a name together brought home the fact that they had equal share in raising their baby. She found herself wondering about forever. That was how she knew she may have fallen a little in love with Ty sometime between their "little something" and now.

She swallowed, reminding her traitorous heart of the brevity of his stay. It would be best to avoid thoughts of any kind of future together. Shifting focus to the minimal furnishing and mostly bare walls, she said, "I like the place. It's nice in a blank canvas sort of way."

Ty chuckled. "Thanks. I think."

"It's not a bad thing. A blank canvas means you can do anything with the place."

"True," he said. "However, there's no point, since this isn't my home."

Despite all the admonishing she'd served her heart, the words stung a little. Did the sentiment refer to the house or the country? Probably both, she told herself, holding on to the disappointment closing in on her. Better to hurt a little for a moment now than a lot forever.

Ty's hands wandered from her face, tweaking her right nipple before settling on her lower abdomen. His touch was so light, as if meant for the baby. Her entire focus converged on his hands, his caress.

"Do you have twins in your family?" he asked.

Patricia twisted herself to look at him. "Twins? Aren't we getting ahead of ourselves?"

He met her chuckle with a grin. "I'm hopeful."

She did a mental search of her extended family. "None I can think of. You?"

He shook his head.

"For someone who didn't plan this, you really seem to be embracing the idea of fatherhood."

He remained quiet, thoughtful, for several moments. "I've always wanted to be a dad. Granted, I didn't think it would happen like this, but it doesn't make me any less excited."

"Twins are an exciting thought, but I'll be happy with one," she said. "I guess we'll find out at my next appointment. I'm supposed to do a scan."

"We? Does this mean I don't have to worm my way into your good graces in order to go with you?"

She hadn't meant it like that, but before now she'd have been on mental alert to avoid any slip ups. Now that "we" had been put out there, she found she didn't mind at all. The truth was, she wanted to share the experience with someone. Normally, she'd have asked Naaki, but her friend had too much on her plate with the wedding. In any case, Ty had every right to be there. Besides, she'd expected him to latch on and railroad her like he'd done with the Cape Coast trip. That he didn't made her answer a simple one.

"Yes."

"Good."

After several minutes of silence, she turned around fully, placing her head on his chest and snuggling closer. His steady heartbeat contrasted with her rapidly escalating one as her mind pondered the possibility of more evenings like this. With a sigh, she pushed the thoughts out of her head, deciding to simply enjoy the moment.

"I like this," she said.

"Me too." He pressed a kiss on her hairline. It seemed such an odd place for a kiss and yet so sweet. After a while, he whispered, "T?"

"Hmm?"

"Look at me."

She gazed up. A shiver snaked down her spine as their eyes held for several seconds. His gaze dropped, and his fingers rose to touch the base of her neck.

"Your heart's racing."

She swallowed. If he kept this up, she'd be in serious trouble because she really liked being with him like this.

"I have a proposition," he said.

Inadvertently, she stiffened. It must have been the incredible gentleness of his tone, the kind of tone a man acquired when he had feelings. *Oh God.* Was he about to say he loved her? How the hell would she respond? She had yet to accept falling for him. She didn't know how she'd react if he told her he loved her. She reached through her mind for something to say, which would prevent him from uttering words she couldn't say back, but the intensity of his gaze froze her, momentarily stole words from her mouth.

He smiled. "Relax, I'm not proposing."

Her momentary panic attack dissipated in a nervous laugh. Did it sound as embarrassed to him as it did to her?

"She breathes a sigh of relief," he teased.

This time, she laughed out loud, even as heat rose up her face. She hoped he didn't sense her embarrassment, but when he tut-tutted, she knew he had.

"I'm mortified."

"You should be," he answered, even though the corners of his lips were still curved upward, then suddenly his brows furrowed. "What did you think I was going to say?"

"I don't know. You looked so serious." No way was she telling him what she'd expected and dreaded. "You accused me once of forever being on the defensive."

"Yes?"

"Maybe that's what it was."

When he still seemed skeptical, she changed tactics. "Hey, I didn't inherit any of my grandaunt's alleged gift of prophesy."

It worked, thankfully. He laughed quietly.

"What's your proposition?"

A beat passed. "Move in with me."

Whoa. Her lips parted then closed without a sound coming out. She pulled back a notch.

"Here me out before you say no," he added quickly. "I was wrong to propose the way I did."

"You were?"

Of course, he was. It only surprised her he'd admitted it.

"You're not a romantic," he continued.

She cocked an eyebrow. *O-k-a-a-y.*

"You're practical," he added. "The flipside of the coin is you think of all the things that could go wrong, and once you see the obstacles, it gets hard to appreciate the possibilities."

She supposed he had a point, but there was nothing wrong with being practical, right? If more people approached life with level-headedness, maybe they'd avoid a lot of heartache.

"Moving in with you sounds more romantic than practical," she commented.

"Not really." He sounded so confident. "Think about it. If you moved in with me, you'd see firsthand how a life together could be."

"I don't know."

She wasn't scandalized by the idea per se. After all, they lived in the twenty-first century and most people had stopped judging such living arrangements negatively. In fact, her mother might even be on board with this crazy proposition, judging by how well she took to Ty. Patricia had no intention of telling her mother, though.

"I'm not asking you to sell or give out your place. You can move out whenever you wish, so don't over-think it."

"I'm not."

This might work to her advantage, she realized. If they lived together, maybe he'd finally see being in each other's face all the time wasn't as romantic as it sounded. Perhaps then, he'd abandon the idea of marriage, and they could go back to their previous no-strings-attached arrangement until he left. This time, she had a few weeks to get used to the idea. They'd have to figure out how to make it work for their child.

He cupped her cheek. "Say yes."

"Okay," she said. "Yes, but only for a week, after which we can discuss it again."

"Really?" He raised his brows. "I expected to spend all night winning you over."

She cocked her brow. "How were you planning on convincing me?"

He winked, lowered his head, and kissed her lightly. "I can think of several things."

She snuggled closer, returning his kiss. "Well, lucky for you, I promised Naaki I'd change my attitude and say yes more often."

"Yeah?"

"Yes."

"Thane and I have a term for that, you know."

"A 'yes day', I know." When he frowned, she added, "Naaki told me about it."

"Is that what this is?"

She nodded. "Are you offended?"

"You're kidding, right? Remind me to thank Naaki for convincing you." He squeezed a little tighter. "I must be one lucky guy for getting to you on your yes day."

"It's actually a yes week."

His look, a combination of surprise and pleasure, was priceless. "A whole week of having to say yes?"

"What can I say? I don't do things by half-measure."

His laugh sounded teasing and maniacal at the same time. "Oh, I'm going to enjoy this."

అంలం

Ty didn't know how long they remained entwined on the couch. Patricia had fallen asleep, and he continued to hold her while listening to her gentle breathing, smiling when she shifted with a whimper and settled into, he assumed, a more comfortable position. For her. Him? He had an erection so hard, it surprised him how he managed to only watch her and stroke her arm when he really wanted to strip her naked and make love to her all night.

His gaze zeroed in on her lips and their enticing pout. His own lips twitched with the temptation to kiss her awake and whisper sweet nothings in her ear until she wanted to make love as badly as he wanted her this moment. Remembering his promise to keep it strictly platonic tonight, he grimaced. What had possessed him to think that would be a good idea? *Oh, yeah*. It came to him instantly. *Forever versus for now.*

With a resigned sigh, he maneuvered himself into a standing position with her still in his arms. He made his way to the bedroom without incident. It wasn't until he stood by the bed, about to lower her onto it that he realized the trap he'd set for himself. For several moments he stood transfixed, a part of him wanting to throw caution to the wind. After all, she had no idea about the promise he'd made. He could break it and recommit in the morning. *No harm done.*

He gave a snort, knowing the damage which could

result from breaking his word, even if said word had been to himself. For one, it would prove Trish's fears right—they couldn't be a normal couple, that all they had was sex.

Besides, his pact had been for one night. He had the rest of the week to make love with her whenever and wherever he wanted. With renewed resolve, he managed to temper down his desire enough to place her on the bed without undressing her.

However, he couldn't resist touching her face, caressing her soft cheeks, and her lips that had driven him to heights of pleasure more times than he could count.

Her eyes fluttered open, focusing on him, and a smile came to her lips. "Sorry I fell asleep on you. I didn't realize how tired I was."

Her groggy-with-sleep voice held a unique appeal, and all his hard work of sticking to his word began to fray at the seams.

"No need to apologize," he said. "Besides, I'm not complaining."

"That's because you don't know what I had planned for tonight."

He raised a brow. "What would that be?"

"Seduction," she whispered in a manner of someone divulging scandalous news.

Though he recognized the humor, Ty couldn't laugh. He swallowed, happy she'd been too tired to seduce him, because any such move from her and he'd have caved like a ton of bricks.

To ensure she didn't wake fully and attempt it now, he moved to the head of the bed, sitting so she lay between his legs.

"You should get some sleep." He cradled her head between his palms, placing his ring and middle fingers against her temples and started a gentle circular motion.

She moaned, shutting her eyes. "Feels good."

Within minutes, she was asleep.

He returned to the living area in a desperate attempt to douse his arousal before going to sleep. He tried watching the news and soon realized he wasn't paying any attention. He needed to talk to someone. His phone screen flashed the time. Eleven o'clock. Too late to call Thane, but it would be barely six p.m. in Massachusetts where his sister lived, and she'd be home from work. He dialed her line from the temporary phone he'd purchased. Special rates to some selected destinations, including the US, made it less expensive to call on a local line than on his US cell phone.

He dialed the number and muted the TV while it rang.

"Hello."

Ty heard the smile in her voice and met it with one of his own. "Hey, Gabs."

"How's the motherland treating you?"

"It's been great."

They spent a few minutes on pleasantries, catching up on each other's lives.

"Are you going to tell me why you called, or do I have to reach through the phone and strangle it out of you?"

Busted.

"Can't I just call my big sister and say hi?"

"Ty, please. Even when you're home, you don't call me twice in one week unless there's something."

"You're right," he said. "Are you sitting down?"

There was a pause.

"Oh God. You're not sick or anything, are you?"

"Sick? That's what comes to mind when your brother calls with news?"

"It's that or you're getting married, and we both

know you're not getting married," she replied. "Wait. Are you?"

Ty decided to cut to the chase. "Not yet, but I met someone."

She gasped. "For real? What's her name?"

Ty smiled. "Patricia Owusu."

"Damn, I should move to Ghana too and find me a man."

"We're having a baby."

"Whoa! How did you get her pregnant so quick?" Gabby asked. "I mean, congratulations?"

"Thanks," he said with a chuckle. "Actually, I met her when I visited before."

"And you kept it all to yourself?"

"I'm a dude. We don't talk about stuff like this unless there's news."

"You're happy about this right? You sound happy."

"Yes, I am," he said. "I think she's the one."

"So, when I said you're getting married, it was actually kind of on the mark."

"If I can convince her to marry me. She has it in her head she's burdening me with this, and it's blinding her from seeing how good we are together."

"Is she crazy? What woman wouldn't want to marry a fine brother like you?"

"Is that sarcasm?"

She snickered. "Seriously, though. Maybe it's a good thing. Gives you a chance to think things through. We both know the value of marrying someone who loves you back and is as committed as you are."

Ty nodded, then realizing she couldn't see, he answered, "I know, but it's not that she isn't committed."

"Does she like you, at least?"

Ty's mind drifted to the image of Trish just before he left her in the bedroom. The fact that she was here and had agreed to stay at least the week told him some of her rules no longer applied to him. "I'd have to say yes."

"Is she against marriage?"

"I don't think so."

"Then what is it?"

"She thinks I'm going to bail on her and the kid."

"Why would she think that?"

Ty sighed, dragging a hand over his face in frustration. "Her dad pulled a mom."

"Oh," was all Gabby said, her tone understanding.

A moment of silence followed.

"On the plus side, she doesn't sound like the type who'd jump ship," Gabby said.

"If only she'd stop trying to toss me overboard."

"If I know my brother, you'll figure something out."

"Already working on it, but I have my work cut out for me. She's stubborn as a mule."

Gabby laughed. "Any woman who has you all worked up like this has my vote. You're too cocky."

Despite himself, Ty laughed, continuing the banter. "Thanks, sis. I needed to be brought down a peg or two."

"Ty, I have to go. Dinner isn't going to make itself."

"Sure thing."

With a promise to call again in a few days, Ty disconnected the call. The conversation with his sister boosted Ty's morale, giving him a general good feeling within. He whistled random tunes while checking the doors and windows. Now he needed to go back to bed and hold the stubborn woman he'd fallen for.

Chapter 17

Patricia woke up at the crack of dawn and instantly became aware of Ty's arms around her, his morning erection nestled against her backside. She lay still, listening to the sound of his relaxed breathing. Her heart seemed to beat in rhythm with his. She couldn't remember the last time she'd woken up buzzing with this much joy. Being able to sleep without setting an alarm, without the need to stay vigilant about returning to her place before morning may have had something to do with it, but Patricia suspected it had more to do with Ty and his TLC.

She'd fallen asleep in his arms last night on the couch. Her heartbeat spiked as she remembered the tender look in Ty's eyes when she'd woken up to find him laying her on the bed. He'd touched her face with such affection she'd expected it to progress to lovemaking. Instead, he'd begun to massage her temples with gentle strokes, lulling her into an immediate state of relaxation and contentment. Sleep had claimed her easily.

She took in a deep breath and released it in a contented sigh. A girl could get used to this. She stiffened. Where had that thought come from? She'd agreed to live with him only because she knew it would be a temporary arrangement. She had no business liking it.

Ty's hand moved to cradle her abdomen and a warm sensation melted within her.

Without warning, emotion constricted her throat. What had she gotten herself into? She should never have agreed to this arrangement. She'd expected it to be a way of getting him out of her system, taking enough of him so she wouldn't need him after he left, but she'd been lying to herself in her attempt to shield her heart from the truth. What she'd thought to be a possibility had now assumed the coat of reality. Ty's second departure would devastate her.

"Good morning, beautiful lady." Ty's voice, an octave lower than usual due to sleep, vibrated against the skin at the base of her neck just before his lips followed. "Sleep well?"

She shuddered. It seemed Ty's effect on her kept getting more potent. She nodded, not trusting her vocal chords to cooperate if she attempted to speak.

"Good," he whispered, planting another kiss on her nape followed by another and another.

She forced her mind not to dwell on the heat expanding from the spot where his hand lay on her stomach or the need pooling in her center.

"The massage you gave me last night was the best I've ever had. No professional can touch your magic hands."

Warm breath fanned her neck when he chuckled. "At your service."

Even in her fogged state, she hadn't missed the deftness of his strokes. Ty had massaged her like a professional. She knew because she was well-versed in massage therapy, but in her case, it was her job.

"Where did you learn?"

"I took a massage therapy course once. I thought it would be a good skill to have."

She turned to look in his eyes. As their gazes locked, a shiver galloped up her body. All these shivers and bated breaths—they were a whole new reaction to Ty. Was it pregnancy hormones?

She didn't want to dwell on other possibilities, so she teased. "I thought accountants are supposed to be boring."

His laugh washed over her like a soothing balm on aching joints. "I'm not your average accountant."

She snuggled closer, her hand caressing one of his well-defined biceps. "Indeed, you're not."

He cupped her cheek, leaned in, and kissed her lightly on the lips. His eyes sparkled with the smile formed on his lips as he traced the outline of her face. For several moments, she stared into his green eyes, enjoying the gentle strokes of his fingers as she also caressed his arms and chest.

"I don't remember the last time I didn't want to get out of bed," she confessed.

A low laugh sounded in his throat. "Last time I visited, you were always up before the alarm. I couldn't help wondering what was wrong with me that made you so eager to get away from me."

"There was absolutely nothing wrong with you."

Her mind went back to those early days. She'd been so focused on upholding her rule of never sleeping over that she hadn't allowed herself to sleep fully. It had been stressful, and perhaps even a bit unsafe for a woman to drive home on her own at midnight, but thankfully Ghana was relatively safe in that regard. If only she'd known how much better the sex could be when you weren't watching the clock and how much more restful sleep was in the arms of a skilled lover.

She nearly winced. Had she devalued what they had by calling it "sleeping in the arms of a skilled lover?" Did their relationship qualify as anything more? Sure, she had Ty's undivided attention now, but the fact remained that he'd taken a break from his regular life. No matter how long he hung around, he'd eventually have to return to America.

Not many men would upend their lives for a woman's sake. Patricia didn't expect or demand it of Ty, though his best friend had done so to be with the woman he loved. Even if Ty offered, she'd have to do the right thing and turn him down. So why did a part of her pray he wouldn't offer to stay? Would she consider it if he did?

No. she wouldn't—couldn't—consider it for her sake and for her child's. She knew how much it scarred a child to wait for a father who never showed up.

"Are you having regrets?" Ty's low voice cut through her thoughts.

She raised her brows. "About?"

"Staying over."

She shook her head, noting the hint of concern in his voice. It would be the first time he'd shown signs of uncertainty about anything. No doubt he wouldn't appreciate her calling it "cute," so she hid the teasing smile tickling the corners of her lips.

"Good." He squeezed her gently. "You looked serious for a while there."

"I was thinking about Naaki." After a moment, she added, "I can't believe she's getting married."

"Thane is one of the most decent guys I know," Ty replied. "I couldn't be happier for him. If you ask me, I don't think either of them had a choice other than to fall in love."

Love. Exactly! Thane had fallen head over heels in love. Not so, Ty. At least he hadn't said it or shown any signs of it. She didn't want him to, anyway.

"They're perfect for each other, aren't they? It's like the universe conspired to bring them together."

Ty pulled back a notch, availing himself of a full view of her face. "I may have been wrong about you. Those are words of a romantic."

"Hey, you're the one throwing about names. I never agreed to not being a romantic."

His laughter draped her in warmth.

After a moment, he said, "Tell me about the suit-case."

"What suitcase?" She frowned, reaching through her mind for a connection. "You mean for the customary marriage ceremony?"

He nodded.

Talk about interesting pillow talk.

"Well," she started, "I guess I should begin by saying our customary weddings kind of reinforce the saying 'a good woman is hard to find,' so as you've already heard, the ceremony gives the groom the avenue to thank the girl's parents for raising a good woman and also to demonstrate his ability to take care of his wife."

"In what way?"

"Gift-giving, which you already know about," she answered. "The groom thanks the parents and the extend-ed family with gifts of money and African wax print cloth. There's a special gift to the bride's brothers called the *akonta sekan*—literally, brother-in-law's sword."

At Ty's raised brows, she explained, "The bride isn't present at the beginning of the ceremony, so after the groom has stated his business, the woman's family goes to fetch her. It's assumed the brother or brothers will use the sword to protect the bride and entourage."

"Where are we going to find a sword?"

The worried look on his handsome face made her laugh.

"It's actually cash these days."

"This is all to thank the family, right? You said something about demonstrating his ability to take care of his wife."

"That's the suitcase. It contains several pieces of wax prints, scarves, shoes, lingerie, and jewelry. A starter wardrobe for his wife-to-be."

He looked as if he wanted to probe further, but eventually just nodded, appearing satisfied with the information she'd given.

"You really are interested in this stuff, aren't you?" she said.

"I am."

"Then here's a piece of trivia you might find interesting. Traditionally, and I mean way back in history, the father of the bride didn't get a full piece of fabric. He got what is called a *danta*."

He smiled, his eyes sparkling with interest. "I'll bite. What's a *danta*?"

"You've obviously seen photos of pre-colonial African men—bare-chested, wearing a piece of cloth over their goods." She waved her hand around Ty's groin area.

He laughed, a full-bodied, head-thrown-back, sexy as hell laugh. She couldn't help smiling, wondering what she'd said that was so funny.

"Care to share the joke?"

"Basically, what Thane should be giving Naaki's dad is a pair of boxers or briefs."

The sound of their laughter surrounded them, filling her with warm cozy sensations. A lump formed in her throat. She could get used to this. Yet being too comfort-able around Ty was the last thing she needed to be think-ing about. She snuggled closer, refusing to dwell on those thoughts. She released a contented sigh against the solid expanse of his chest. He wrapped his arms around her.

"You're different," she said.

"Different than whom?"

She shrugged. "Other men."

His chest jerked as though he'd chuckled, though she heard no sound. She'd expected him to probe further, but he didn't. Instead, he released a deep breath and pressed a kiss onto the crown of her head, tightening his arms around her.

She knew for sure she was in trouble when the sim-ple gesture had her heart melting like ice-cream on a hot West African afternoon. No words he could utter would have affected her as much. *Crap.*

ℰᴕℰᴕ

Two days later, Ty woke up to an empty bed. The sunlight streaming in through the open window and the sounds carrying over from outside told him he'd slept well past his normal wake-up time. His body felt so re-laxed, his heart so content, he didn't feel like getting out of bed anytime soon. The lightness swirling inside his body had everything to do with Trish.

With a smile, he reached for her. His hand found on-ly the empty space she'd occupied only a few hours earli-er. Immediately, his heart's tempo increased to an anx-ious staccato. Had she left in the middle of the night without him sensing her departure? Normally, he was a light sleeper, especially when he had the company of a woman in his bed. That he hadn't heard her get out of bed confirmed her effect on him. This would have worried him if he wasn't sure his heart beat only for her, but Ty knew without a doubt that no woman had ever or would ever affect him the way Patricia did.

Thankfully, the task of convincing her seemed to have taken off smoothly. That is, if she hadn't had a change of heart and sneaked out on him.

He got out of bed and slipped on his boxers. Stomping over to the door, he yanked it open and stopped short at the sound reaching his ears—an enchanting voice, humming a song unfamiliar to him. He did recognize the voice, though, and smiled. He'd never heard her sing before, and as he absorbed its quality, his stomach growled drawing his attention to the aroma of food tickling his nostrils.

He followed the sound and smell, only stopping when he reached the entrance to the kitchenette. Taking full advantage of the fact that she had her back to him, Ty leaned against the wall, admiring the gentle sway of her hips as she danced to her own tune while attending to something on the stove. A smile crept to his lips as he considered the merits and demerits of walking up behind her and squeezing her perfectly shaped ass. Perhaps not a good idea, he conceded, since she was working with hot oil.

Reluctantly, he made his presence known by speaking. "How long have you been awake?"

She started and turned with a gasp then giggled when their eyes met. The sound went right down to his heart.

"You're awake," she said.

He ignored the stirring in his boxers. "I didn't hear you wake up."

"I was very quiet. You looked so peaceful, I made sure I didn't wake you."

"Yeah, I was completely out, but you're good at sneaking out of beds."

Ty could have kicked himself, and he noticed the slight drop in her smile.

"That didn't come out right," he started.

"No need to apologize," she cut in, giving him a brief smile, both of which made him want to go on his knees and beg her forgiveness.

"What are you making?" he asked instead.

Her dazzling smile returned. "*Hausa koko* and *togbe*."

"I'm not even going to try and pronounce those on an empty stomach."

She laughed as she returned her attention to the stove and scooped out tennis-ball sized golden brown donuts.

"I bought the *Hausa koko*, which is millet porridge from Northern Ghana, at the junction, and I'm frying the *togbe*, which are basically donuts."

"They don't look like the ones you made the other day."

"It's a slightly different recipe," she said.

"What ingredients do you use? I'm positive I don't have any here."

"Flour, yeast, nutmeg. I passed by home yesterday to get them," she said. "The rest you had here. Milk and sugar."

She turned off the flame and took out the last batch of donuts from the oil. He assisted in setting the table before they sat down to eat.

"I must warn you, I'm not a huge fan of porridge," Ty said. "Or of big breakfasts as a matter of fact, but—"

She didn't let him finish. "It's Ghanaian, and so you'll try it without any bias."

He chuckled. He and Patricia had hit it off from the start, but this sort of banter was a new space.

"I was gonna say, you cooked it, so I'm going to eat it without complaining."

"That's sweet, but don't suffer in silence on my account. If you hate it, I can boil water for coffee."

As she spoke, she gave his hand a light squeeze. The gesture seemed so natural, like something an old couple would do. He liked this new space in which they found themselves. They were only two days into their living together arrangement, and he had no idea how it would go.

Normally, when it came to risk, both in life and in business, the accountant in him took dominance, forcing him to err on the side of caution. For some reason, when it came to Patricia, the cautious side of him seemed to give way to his risk-taking side. He shouldn't count his chickens before they hatched, yet he couldn't help raising his expectations about the outcome of his plan.

First, he sampled the *togbe*, which he liked, then spooned some *Hausa koko* into his mouth. He took a moment to savor the burst of flavors. He whistled, sucking in air at the unexpected spiciness flaming his mouth.

"Is there ginger in this?" he asked.

She nodded. "There's probably pepper too. Is it too much? Should I get you water?"

He shook his head. "Woman, I can handle spice."

She raised a brow and her lips twitched with a laugh she tried to suppress.

"It's not unbearable," he explained. "Just unexpected."

"How did you guess ginger and not hot pepper?"

"I'm a bit of a foodie," he confessed. "I can often ID ingredients in a meal." He noted her raised eyebrows. "Impressed?"

"I am. What else can your superior taste buds make out?"

"I wish I could attribute it to superior taste buds, but the truth is far less glamorous," he answered with a short laugh. "I bussed tables in my teens, and the chef liked to experiment with new recipes and spices. I was his willing guinea pig."

The glow of admiration in her eyes didn't diminish. "It's still remarkable."

His heart swelled in response to her compliment as he obliged her request with a couple more scoops of the porridge. "Cloves? Maybe nutmeg, but that could be from the donuts."

The light-hearted conversation continued as they completed breakfast.

"What's your day like today?" Ty asked.

"Just the photoshoot," she said, and when he frowned, she added, "Didn't I mention I'm handling the make-up for Naaki and Thane's ad?"

He shook his head. "I know about the photoshoot, but not about you working on the set."

"What about you?" she asked.

Mentally, he rearranged his schedule for the day. "As it turns out, I'm coming to the set too."

She gave him a smile that set his heart racing. He fought the temptation to coerce her into ditching the job and spending the day at home with him…in bed…or maybe on the couch…or kitchen counter…

All the above?

"What's funny?"

He shook his head. This must be the definition of madness. Addiction, he corrected. Something about Trish connected with him on a primal level. It was probably the reason, she'd stuck in his mind the whole time he'd been back in the US, and even more so now that he'd gotten to know her better. Now that she was having his baby.

"I'm just happy I get to witness you doing your thing. It might even give me ideas to help you with your business plan."

"That reminds me. I have a full draft now."

"I can't wait to look at it."

Her smile brightened further, if it were possible, but she didn't otherwise respond.

Staring into her eyes, he couldn't help sending up a prayer. After the past two days, he had little doubt this experiment would open Trish's eyes and make her see their relationship in terms of forever instead of just for now, but he wasn't ashamed to ask for divine help.

Eventually, when he proposed again, she would have no choice but to say yes.

Chapter 18

Patricia had worked on beauty pageants, weddings, and a lot of other events, but never an advertising campaign, and as those went, this would be huge. It was a cookbook showcasing local recipes from all over West Africa along with tips for food presentation, which would be unique, since local cuisine relied on the cook's experience in gauging the correct levels of spices and ingredients. This cookbook would revolutionize cooking of indigenous dishes.

It seemed the client spared no expense in this three-hundred-and-sixty-degree campaign, which in layman's language meant they were doing the whole shebang—TV and radio ads, posters and billboards, and a host of social media. They were calling it the *Art You Can Eat* campaign.

This week, they were filming teasers to be launched on TV and YouTube, so it was a relatively small set with only three models for Patricia to work on.

"Tell me again why you guys are filming this so

close to your wedding," Patricia said to Naaki as she worked on the first model.

They were in the dressing room, one of the offices at Media Image Advertising—MIA.

"Volta Foods wants to launch the cookbook in March in time for pre-Easter spending, so the teaser campaign must be launched ASAP."

"Thank goodness. I thought you two were just workaholics," Patricia said, but stuck out her tongue. "I'd be disappointed to find out you spent your honeymoon brainstorming new campaigns."

"I don't know where you get the notion Thane and I are workaholics."

"Need I remind you how this idea of *art you can eat* came about?"

Truth be told, it was a romantic story. Thane had been down with malaria and Naaki had gone visiting. While nursing him back to health, they had somehow got talking about work and come up with the idea for the campaign. Either way, Patricia suspected that night had marked the real moment when Naaki and Thane's relationship had shifted from business to personal.

"We only had a work relationship at the time."

"Until you woke up in his arms the next morning."

Naaki grinned, rolling her eyes. "The reason we want to do this now is so we don't have to think about it on our honeymoon."

"If you say so."

The playful banter continued as Patricia completed the make-up for all three models.

They then proceeded to the creative studio, where a kitchen had been set up. For all intents and purposes, it appeared to be an ultra-modern kitchen, but when you went behind the counter, it was made mostly of plywood.

The moment they walked into the studio, Patricia's

gaze sought Ty. She found him sitting in one corner of the room with Thane. He smiled and waved. Her heart did a flip as she returned the wave and set up her tools on a table provided in another corner of the room where she could touch up the make-up between takes.

She watched as Thane kissed the air, and Naaki reached up to catch it. The diamond stud on her engagement ring sparkled.

"I can't believe you're getting married. Now I'll have no partner for our usual thirty-first December thing."

"We can make it a pre-thirty-first thing from now on, or you can join Thane and me to usher in the new year."

"Please, I have no desire to be a third wheel," Patricia said. "Besides, everyone knows a newlywed couple needs to enjoy each other during their first year, including celebrating special occasions as a couple without having to entertain best friends."

Naaki flashed one of her I'm-so-in-love smiles. "December is a long way off. Who knows, with the looks you and Ty have been exchanging, you two may be together-together by then."

"You're such a romantic. Ty and I will never be together-together."

"Then why are you staying with him?"

"It's only for this week, thanks to you," Patricia said. "I'm just doing it to prove to him we aren't meant to be together."

Her best friend looked doubtful. "You moved in with him—"

"Only for the week," Patricia stressed.

"Fine, only for a week," Naaki conceded, "to prove that marrying him would be a bad idea?"

"When you put it like that—"

"Meanwhile he thinks he's going to convince you of

the opposite?" When Patricia nodded, Naaki asked, "Who's winning so far?"

Patricia's mind played back the past couple of days with Ty. Things had been going well. Too well. This worried her. She'd expected the arrangement to be a big failure. Being up in each other's faces should have exposed them to each other's vices, which she'd hoped would put Ty off. Even within her, a war raged between her head and her heart. Waking up wrapped in his arms, leaving home and returning together, spending a good part of the night making love and pillow-talking before drifting off to bed didn't exactly spell doom and gloom.

If the past two days were anything to go by, then convincing him marriage wasn't the solution to their predicament would be that much harder.

"It's too early to tally points," she said.

"In other words, Ty, one." Naaki linked her thumb and forefingers to form a zero. "Patricia, nil."

Patricia didn't respond, but her gaze drifted back to Ty who chatted with Thane. She found herself thrust again into thoughts of him. Ty had to be the only man on earth who remembered to put down the toilet seat. The few not-so-great things—like when he made his coffee boiling hot and had to slurp the first few sips or his insistence on squeezing the toothpaste anywhere his hand touched—only came as a reminder he wasn't perfect. Which, oddly, made her like him even more.

Her best friend had a point. If this were a contest, she was definitely losing.

e✧∽e✧∽

Ty sensed the now familiar heat of awareness and knew Patricia was looking at him again. He found himself only half-listening to Thane's explanation about something wedding-related. She turned away abruptly the moment he looked up and a smile came to his lips. He watched, engrossed at the way she kept fiddling with a strand of her braids. He couldn't wait to dip his hands in there and bring her lips to his.

She looked up again and this time smiled before shifting her attention to something Naaki said. She looked particularly fetching in a black pencil skirt and a loose African print top and matching headgear. From across the room, he couldn't read the expression in her eyes, yet each time their gazes collided he wondered if she could see right into his soul.

"You haven't stopped staring at her since she walked in."

Thane's voice reeled Ty out of his trance.

Ty let out an embarrassed laugh. "That obvious, huh?"

"What did you call me before?" Thane said then snapped his fingers. "Whipped. Now who's whipped?"

"Shut up."

Thane laughed. "Mom sends her greetings, by the way. I spoke with her last night."

"How's the old lady?" Ty asked with a smile, knowing Celeste Aleksander would kill him if she ever heard him call her old.

"Eager to meet her future daughter-in-law," Thane said with a smile. "Looks like Naaki's magic isn't meant for just me."

"You're a lucky man," Ty said. "Then again, your mother has a big heart."

"I concur."

Ty's mind drifted to their first summer in college when Thane had invited him to spend the break with his family. Thane's parents had welcomed Ty, their openness somewhat lifting the cloud of dissociation he could never seem to shake. It had been a bittersweet moment. On one hand, Ty had soaked up their affection like a dry sponge absorbs water, on the other hand, their love served as a reminder of the father he'd lost and the mother who'd abandoned him and his sister.

Thane smiled. "Naaki was nervous about meeting her, but after they video chatted the first time, they hit it off like a house on fire."

Ty nodded, unsurprised. Thane's fiancée had the same kind heart Celeste Aleksander possessed. His friend couldn't have picked a better match.

"Can I ask a question?" He didn't wait for a response before continuing. "Ever wonder where you'd be now if you'd never made the move to explore Africa or if your former bosses weren't the shitheads they turned out to be?"

Thane smiled. "You'd still be trying to hook me up with girls called Bubble-gum."

Ty chuckled. "She was called Candy, and I already apologized for that, man. Let it go."

Thane became serious after a moment. "To be honest, I can't even imagine a scenario in which she and I never met. I'm positive fate would somehow have brought us together."

Ty nodded without responding as his gaze trailed back to Patricia. Could fate be working in the background to change her mind?

"Is there something you're not telling me?" Thane asked.

"You mean apart from the baby?"

"What baby?"

Ty returned his gaze to his friend and noted the total confusion on Thane's face. "Oh, shit. I assumed you knew by now."

A lightbulb seemed to go off in Thane's mind as understanding took over the initial frown. "You and Patricia are having a baby?"

Ty nodded.

A few seconds elapsed.

Thane exhaled with a low whistle. "Are you okay with that?"

Ty couldn't help smiling. "I'm very okay with it."

"Does she feel the same way?"

Ty let out a breath. "I think so."

Thane raised his brows askance.

"It's complicated."

As he was about to continue, one of the crew called to Thane, asking for some direction on the photoshoot and Thane excused himself to go sort out the issue.

Ty's mood remained contemplative as he took a swig of his drink. Thane's question continued to swirl around in his mind. *Does she feel the same way?* Truth? He had no idea. The fact that she'd decided to keep the baby should mean something. Even pushing him away seemed to be her roundabout way of protecting the baby. *Their* baby. On some level, she had to at least have made peace with the turn of events. They may not have planned it, but he knew without a doubt, given a second chance he'd want both Patricia and their baby in his life. But what would Patricia's choice be if she were given a do-over?

ଔଈଔ

They were on their lunchtime break and Patricia had skipped the group lunch in favor of a sandwich with juice she'd brought from home, and a power nap in the dressing room. Although she'd spent a good portion of the time in the studio sitting down, she'd been called upon several times to touch up the make-up.

It was sweltering outside, and even with the AC

cranked up, it seemed to be a losing battle against the hot weather and the heat emitted by the lights, cameras, and people.

They said the camera added ten pounds. It also magnified the appearance of oily T-zones. This meant Patricia had to be on her feet several times, making sure the models' faces were flawless throughout the shoot.

Fifteen minutes into the powernap, her phone rang. She groaned, picking it up with every intention of cutting it with one of the pre-set SMS responses like "busy, call back later."

When she saw Ty's name in the caller ID, her heart sped with excitement. How could she be so excited at the prospect of hearing his sexy voice when she'd spoken with him less than thirty minutes ago? She popped in her Bluetooth headset and pressed the answer button.

"Hi."

"Are you okay? Naaki said you were tired."

"Yes, I just needed to lie down. I'll be out in a moment."

"No," he said. "We still have another fifteen minutes until we reconvene, but if you're well rested there's something else I'd like to ask. Are you well-rested?"

"Yes. Why?"

"Is there are mirror in there?"

She frowned, mild suspicion lacing her brows as her gaze trailed to the full-length mirror to her left. "Yes, why?"

"Good."

Her curiosity aroused, she asked, "Ty, what's this about?"

"I want you to do something special for me," he said in a deep, low voice full of mischief and her body began to tingle. "Take off your panties, sit in front of the mirror, and spread your legs."

She sucked in a breath at the sexy command. "Wh—what?"

Although she knew she was alone, Patricia cast a quick glance around.

He repeated his words, injecting a breathy quality to his voice as he enunciated each word.

"I can't," she said. "Someone could walk in here any minute."

"Not when I'm standing guard."

She gasped. "You're at the door?"

"Your personal bodyguard."

Arousal pulsed in her core, yet she hesitated. "Ty—"

He spoke at the same time. "Remember you can't say no."

She swallowed. *Damn yes week.*

His voice held a hint of amusement and a whole lot of spice, and her knees went weak. Yet her hands made no move to rid her of her panties nor did her legs propel her toward the mirror. A part of her questioned her hesitation. It wasn't as if she wasn't already aroused. All it took was his sensual let's-get-it-on voice to get her there. His sexy command, coupled with his voice in her ear and the knowledge of his nearness, only fanned the flames of need moving her from want to yearn within a matter of seconds as evidenced by her already damp panties and pebbled nipples.

She thought of the times she'd pleasured herself during the last three months thinking about Ty and imagining his hands on her. She didn't know why, but her heart pounded with a certainty that doing this would shift the dynamics of their relationship. Could she handle Ty getting any further under her skin?

"Trish?"

His voice strummed her desire as if he'd touched her. "Okay."

The singular word had tumbled out of her mouth sealing her decision.

Moments later, she stood in front of the mirror. With fingers trembling from the combination of her arousal and her increasing excitement at doing something naughty, she lifted her skirt and slipped off her panties. Then she lowered herself on to the stool in front of the mirror. Slowly, she parted her legs.

"Done."

"Use your fingers, honey. I want you to see your arousal."

Her breath hitched as she slipped her ring and fore fingers between her nether lips, spreading them until she was fully exposed.

"Done," she said in a breathy voice.

"Good girl," he whispered, as if he could see her.

The door remained shut, so the possibility that he could see her was next to nil, yet the notion of it brought a delicious ache to her core that demanded immediate attention.

"Tell me how wet you are."

Her middle finger touched her center, sliding over her swollen bud and she gasped at the shock of electricity.

"So wet…" she moaned.

"Pleasure yourself for me."

She rubbed her love button, slick with her intimate juices.

"Does it feel good?"

"Oh, Ty," she breathed. "Yes."

He groaned. "Honey, I'm so hard for you right now."

Oh. His low growl in her ear heightened her pleasure and her finger moved faster, coaxing her hips to join in the dance. She wanted to tell him to come in and take her fully, but the words caught in her throat, and the only sound emanating from her were deep moans of pleasure.

"Stroke your nipples."

Her free hand slid under her top tweaking her nipple through her bra with more enthusiasm than planned. Pleasure and pain shot through her, making her gasp. Her fingers worked simultaneously on her clit and her nipple extracting deep moans from her. All the while Ty whispered endearments in her ear.

Her release rushed at her.

"You're beautiful," he whispered, as he often did when he was looking into her eyes when making love with her.

"Ty…" she groaned just before tumbling into oblivion.

Her legs trembled as her inner muscles continued to contract with remnants of her release.

"Ty? Are you still there?"

"Yes, Trish."

"Come in. I want you inside me."

"If I come in now, we won't be done before someone comes searching for us," he said. "But hold that thought. I'll be inside you tonight."

With that, he clicked off, leaving her sated and wanting, and incredibly pissed all at the same time.

Chapter 19

The rest of the afternoon went by excruciatingly slowly. The entire time Ty couldn't stop thinking about what had transpired between him and Patricia during the lunch break. He was paying the price too, having to put every ounce of effort into keeping his thoughts and desire in check. Not an easy feat since he couldn't seem to take his eyes off her for more than a few seconds at a time. Neither did it help when he found her stealing glances at him as well.

Even amid people, the sizzling electricity crackled between them. By the time the photoshoot ended, he yearned to haul Patricia out of there and get started on the sensual promise he'd made.

Thane and Naaki invited them for an early dinner, which they both declined, Patricia claiming fatigue and Ty begging off with the excuse of making sure she got home safe and sound. The raised eyebrows from their best friends clearly said they didn't buy the stories, but they were gracious enough to accept the excuses.

Once in Patricia's car, which had finally returned from the workshop, they'd giggled like two teenagers. They bought pizza on the way, because they didn't plan on cooking or going out once they reached home. The moment they entered the house, they tossed the pizza box on the kitchenette counter and fell into each other's arms.

They didn't make it past the living room, as with frenzied hands they ridded themselves of the inhibitions of clothes.

The sex was hot and heady, without preamble. The quick release energized them as they moved it to the bathroom where they washed down and made love again in the shower. By the time they got to the bedroom, the urgency had dissipated, allowing them to slow down and indulge in each other until they lay side-by-side, sated and boneless.

Patricia had made a pillow of Ty's torso, while stroking his chest hair with her delicate fingers. Like a balloon, Ty's heart seemed to expand with each stroke until, at a point, he feared it would burst.

Taking in a deep breath, he maneuvered himself until he was propped up on one elbow and she lay in the crook of his arm, staring into his eyes. The atmosphere between them still sizzled. Instead of quenching their desires, their lovemaking had only stoked the embers further. They would need all night, but for now he satisfied himself with staring at her.

"It was incredible," Patricia said.

"Which part?" Ty asked, trying to lighten the mood a bit, because his heart had begun beating to a new tune.

"The whole show," she said with a mischievous smile as though there were some hidden meaning in her words.

He was in no state of mind to decipher any cryptic messages, so he settled for a kiss. As he pulled away, their gazes locked, and his heart did the balloon thing again.

"I can't get enough of you," he whispered.

So many words swirled around in his mind all echoing one thing. *Love.* He sucked in a breath, letting it sink in, imbue every pore and fiber of his body. In the sensual silence engulfing them, he gazed at her unable to mask what lay in his heart.

"Ty, what is it?"

She touched his face, searching, and he sensed she could see it in his eyes; the unspoken words at the tip of his tongue, words he'd never told any other woman before, but he knew them to be true. He loved her.

"Trish, I—"

"I'm—" she started at the same time.

A giggle broke out from her, but he couldn't shift gears fast enough to join in.

"You first," he said.

"I'm starving," she answered.

He swallowed back the disappointment seeping into his mood, desperately wanting to go back to cuddling and pleasurable silence.

He drew in a long breath and pulled out of her arms.

"Wait here." He got out of the bed. "I'll warm the pizza and bring it."

She nodded, and he started to leave.

"Ty," she called back.

He turned and paused, drinking her in. She sat with her legs crossed, hands by her sides, her perky breasts standing proud, beckoning him.

"What were you going to say?"

He stared into her eyes, heart racing. Worry stole into him. God, who would have thought Ty Webber would lose his nerve in front of the woman he loved?

He shook his head. "It can wait."

Something has changed.

Those words swirled around in Patricia's head as she sat staring at the door missing Ty's warm embrace. She knew exactly when it happened. After all, it was her fault. They were basking in the sweet aftermath of their love-making, and for the first time ever, she'd stopped worrying about what anything meant and simply enjoyed being in his arms, content without reservation.

Then he'd risen over her and stared into her eyes. She was used to the intensity of his shocking green gaze particularly during and shortly after sex, but tonight there had been something else, something she hadn't seen in his eyes before, so when he'd opened his mouth to speak, she'd panicked and blurted out the first thing that popped into her mind.

For a moment, she'd even thought, "whew, good save," but several minutes later as they shared pizza and juice in bed, she couldn't shake off the niggling curiosity or the notion of having missed something important.

"You okay?" he asked.

His gentle tone bathed her in warmth and an odd sensation filled her chest. It had started this afternoon, after the dressing room incident.

She nodded, because she had food in her mouth and more so because she didn't trust her voice to come out without a tremor. She chased down the food with a sip of her juice.

Her mind drifted to this afternoon in the dressing room, how after a moment, in her mind, it hadn't been her but him touching her. The proof lay in the intensity of her orgasm. She'd never come apart like that at her own hands, and she knew the difference had been Ty. Since then, each time he spoke or looked in her eyes, her heart squeezed or shuddered or did a range of other things she didn't know hearts could do. Finally, she fully accepted the truth she'd attempted to deny all this time. She'd fallen in love with Ty, and it scared the hell out of her.

"This pizza could use a bit of hot pepper," she said, bringing her mind back to the present.

He chuckled. "Ghanaians and your love for spicy food."

"We give the Indians a run for their money."

They settled in companionable silence as they continued to eat.

After a moment, Ty said, "Tell me something funny you did as a kid."

She raised an eyebrow. He'd been doing that all week, asking her questions about herself and her childhood. In the past four days she'd revealed more about herself to him than she'd done with anyone else—aside from Naaki, that is. He'd also revealed things about himself, something that should worry her, because the more she discovered about him, the more she liked him. She caught herself on a few occasions considering the pros and cons of a long-distance relationship until she remembered she wasn't in this alone. Protecting her child, making sure he or she didn't suffer the constant heartache of waiting for a father as she had, superseded her needs.

She pushed aside the thoughts, as she considered his question. She finally settled on something.

"When I was about ten years old, I wrote a will."

With quirked brows he asked, "Why?"

"I thought I was going to die."

He became serious. "Were you ill or something?"

"No," she replied. "I loved guava—I still do—and my mum used to warn me not to swallow the seeds. She told me the seeds would slip into my appendix, and I'd get appendicitis and die. One day, I mistakenly swallowed a seed, so I thought I was going to die and I had to make sure they gave my favorite doll to my best friend."

Ty burst into laughter and Patricia found herself joining in.

"When did you find out you weren't dying?"

"A couple of days later when I mustered the courage to break the news to my mother."

It took a while before Ty's laughter died down. "Good one."

"Your turn," she said.

"Nothing as interesting as writing a will at age ten." He furrowed his brows for a few seconds. "Here we go. In junior high, I used to sneak into the science lab and release all the frogs from being used for dissection."

It was her turn to laugh as she imagined the scene.

"Did you get caught?"

"Let's just say I did detention more times than I care to admit."

They continued to trade childhood stories until they'd emptied the pizza box. Finally, Patricia asked what she'd been dying to ask the whole time.

"What were you going to say earlier? Before you went for the food."

He looked at her, his almost empty glass of juice paused in mid-air. Her heart pounded as she tried but failed to read his expression. He pulled her into his arms and pressed his lips against her temple.

"It's not urgent," he replied.

Disappointment washed over her, but she decided it wise to not press him. He'd tell her when he was ready. Besides, she had no reason to believe she'd like what he had to say. Still, she couldn't shake the feeling that a chasm had suddenly materialized between them.

ഇൗ

The weekend arrived too quickly for Ty's liking, signaling the end of Patricia's yes week, and the leeway he'd had for the past seven days. The past week had been nothing short of perfection. Sure, they'd had one or two disagreements but nothing major, nothing signifying they couldn't weather the storms of life together. If anything, this week had proven beyond doubt they could make a go of it.

However, as much as they complemented each other, he knew living together for one week wouldn't be enough to convince her to marry him. Maybe that accounted for the unease within him since waking up this morning. He needed to keep the momentum going, needed to keep her close for longer, which meant the time had come to kick-start the next phase of his plan.

Right now, though, he needed to get through a game of golf with Thane and Naaki's brother, Nii. They'd agreed to have a guys' only time while Patricia and the rest of the bride's entourage went for a mock make-up session.

"I didn't know mock bridal make-up existed," Ty said, as he prepared to tee off.

Thane laughed. "I'd never heard of it before, but then I've never been married before."

"If you ask me, women make too much fuss over weddings," Nii said. "If I had my way, I'd opt for just the traditional marriage ceremony and a court registration. No fuss, no hassle."

"Good luck with that, man," Ty said. "Women love the fairy-tale. My sister has had a storyboard of ideas for her wedding since she turned sixteen."

"I hear you," Nii said. "In Ghana, there's a whole religious angle attached to it, you don't want to get me started."

Ty nodded, adjusting his cap and wiping sweat off

his forehead. "Since I'm here for a few months, I'm sure I'll find out soon enough."

Thane raised his brows. "A few months? I thought you were booked to return a couple of days after the wedding."

"Change of plans," Ty replied. "I'm staying until the baby comes."

"I'm sure Patricia will be happy to have you around for that."

"Patricia? As in my sister's best friend?" Nii asked.

"The very same," Thane answered.

"You're lucky you aren't related to my sister."

Ty frowned. "How's that?"

"The first time she brought Patricia home, I made the mistake of asking if she was single. Naaki warned me not to even think about asking her friend out unless I planned on marrying her."

"Whoa. That's a tough one." Ty laughed, though he couldn't be certain whether it was at Nii's comment or at himself.

For a moment there, he'd worried Nii and Patricia had been together before. It wouldn't be an issue, of course. She was with Ty now, and he was man enough to stay the hell away from her past relationships even if said past relationship happened to be with his best friend's soon-to-be brother-in-law.

Thane laughed. "I believe you. Naaki gave me a dressing down the day we met for mistakenly hitting someone with a banana peel."

Nii nodded. "Classic Naaki. Thank you for taking her off my family's hands."

As Thane and Nii went off on a tangent discussing Naaki's quirks, Ty's mind drifted to the woman who dominated his thoughts and emotions. She'd need someone to be there for her as the pregnancy progressed. So tonight, he planned on asking her to extend her stay at his place.

He hadn't told her yet about remaining in Ghana until the baby came, but he'd already adjusted the departure on his ticket. *Actions speak louder than words.* The saying had never held truer than in the case of dealing with Patricia.

Ty put his hands together in a time-out gesture. "Guys, we're supposed to be having guy time and we're talking about women."

The other two agreed that the rest of the game should be played without any more talk about the women or the wedding.

A couple of hours later, when they finished their game, they headed toward the parking lot.

"We should do this more often," Nii suggested and Thane agreed.

Just as Nii started saying something again, his phone rang. He fished it out of the gym bag.

"It's my mother," he said. "I'll talk to you guys later."

They said their goodbyes and parted ways.

"Let's hear it," Thane said the moment Nii went out of earshot.

"Nothing to spill."

"At least tell me what Patricia said when you told her you were staying."

"I haven't told her yet."

Thane stopped. "Keeping secrets?"

"It's a surprise. I'm telling her tonight."

Thane raised his brows but didn't respond. As they approached the car, Thane deactivated the alarm, and held the button down to automatically roll down the windows.

Even so, they had to open the doors for a few

minutes to let out the pent-up heat in the car before sitting in.

"Patricia and I are good," Ty found himself saying as they maneuvered out of the lot.

"I didn't say anything."

"You didn't have to."

"Fine," Thane said. "What arrangements are in place for your firm and your clients?"

"I wrapped up quite a few things before heading out here, but whatever comes up, Gill and Masterson can step up."

"Then what?"

"What's with the third degree?"

Thane looked contrite. "I'm sorry, man. I didn't mean to push. It's not like you to make such big decisions on a whim."

"Trust me, I'm not. I've thought long and hard about this. I just need to figure out how to split my time between Ghana and the US for the foreseeable future."

For now, he planned on adjusting his schedule, so he could spend half the year in Ghana and the other half in the States. He had yet to decide which half of the year would be allocated to Ghana and vice versa.

"You've always talked about setting up here. I guess the time has finally come."

Ty nodded.

"Then I suppose I should tell you *akwaaba*."

Ty had Thane drop him off at a flea market he'd seen advertised on Facebook. He planned on getting something nice for Patricia. He spent twenty minutes visiting various stalls and checking out the products before making up his mind on what to get. Finally, he settled on a jar of unprocessed cocoa butter, which he'd seen her use, and some essential oils. A massage tonight wouldn't be out of place.

Just as he paid for the products, his phone beeped with a message, reeling him out of his sensual thoughts before he'd fully slipped into it.

When are you coming home?

A smile touched his lips as he responded.

Soon, honey. Just picking up a few things from the flea market. Are you done with your mock make-up?

Yes.

See you soon.

e/ɔe/ɔ

Patricia's phone rang just as she placed it on the table. She smiled, picking it up, assuming it would be Ty calling. However, the number flashing on the screen didn't look familiar. Hopefully, a referral from one of her clients.

"Hello?"

"Good afternoon, madam. My name is Sandra Sarfo. Am I, please, speaking with Ms. Patricia Owusu?"

"Yes, this is she."

"Did you submit a proposal for the African Women Entrepreneurs Development Fund to help you expand your business?"

Patricia perked up immediately. "Yes, I did."

She hadn't expected to hear anything for a couple of months, since she'd only applied last week. Her heart sank. Did a call this early mean she'd failed the first round?

"We need to confirm some information to complete processing your application," the caller said.

She relaxed, but only a fraction. "Certainly."

"Your application says you have no children, however your proposal suggests you're a single mother."

She released a breath, shifting into sales-pitch mode.

If this conversation had a bearing on her selection, then she had to ace it.

"I'm expecting," she explained. "My proposal takes that into consideration."

"Ah. I see."

Worry crept in. "Is that a problem?"

"On the contrary, madam. The primary aim of this grant is to support single women, and, in particular, single mothers, and enable them to be self-reliant."

Phew. "Okay."

She thought about Ty and how excited he'd be to know she might get a grant for her business.

"May I confirm that you're unmarried at this time?" the lady asked.

"Yes, I'm single." A sense of discomfort settled in Patricia's gut. "Will that affect my chances?"

"Not at all. This year's call is specifically aimed at supporting single mothers and women who don't have a strong nuclear family or other financial support."

Before Patricia could respond, the other lady continued.

"Thank you for your time, Ms. Owusu. Best of luck with the application."

Before she knew it, the call had ended. Patricia frowned. What did this mean? For several seconds she stared straight ahead, worry coiling around her insides as her mind assimilated the implications of the caller's last words. Being with Ty could mean losing out on this opportunity. Sure, there were other means of getting capital, but this grant would mean getting the needed funds without having to pay interest. She needed only to adhere to a list of conditions.

She shook her head. *I'm getting ahead of myself.* This call only signified they'd received her application, not a guarantee of sponsorship.

Why then did her heart continue pounding a nervous beat?

She stared at the phone again, Ty's last text message swirling through her mind. She'd been looking forward to this evening. Heart sinking, she realized her plans had to change. She needed space and a clear head to consider her options. Staying here with Ty would only bias her decision.

Her chest constricted, giving in to numbness, as if her heart had been replaced by a metal ball. Standing, she forced her feet to take her to the bedroom where she proceeded to pack her belongings.

Chapter 20

"Honey, I'm home," Ty called out the moment he crossed the threshold and chuckled at the silliness of it.

He didn't care, though. Like his aunt used to say, "Find a woman you can be yourself with." That was exactly how he felt with Patricia. She was always so open and honest, she'd easily made him shed any form of pretense when it came to her.

He frowned a little when he heard nothing. "T?"

"In here."

Her tone of voice didn't echo his enthusiasm. He chucked it to fatigue. She'd been pushing herself on wedding activities. He needed to remind her to take it easy.

He found her in the living room area and stopped short. She sat in a chair, her back ramrod straight, her hands cupping her knees in a tight grip. His gaze zoomed in to the valise beside her, and all his elation died away.

She stood so fast he feared she might get dizzy. She didn't, so he reined in his need to rush to her aid.

"Going somewhere?"

"Home." Her voice came out hoarse and she cleared her throat. "My place has been unoccupied the entire week."

"You want us to move there? Is that it?"

She shook her head. "Ty, I agreed to staying together only for one week."

"After which you said we'd discuss it," he replied, reminding her of her own words.

"I've thought about it."

"Without giving me the courtesy of offering my opinion?"

She looked away, not giving a response.

A combination of frustration and anger slammed into him, and he fought to keep them at bay, because there had to be a reasonable explanation for her behavior. Carefully, he placed the shopping bag from the flea market on the center table, buying time. When he faced her again, he'd reeled in his emotions.

"What's really going on here, Trish? Did something happen when you were out with the ladies?"

"Nothing happened."

He took a step toward her, but she retreated folding her arms around her midsection in a defensive stance.

"T, talk to me," he said. "If it's something I did, I'm sorry."

She shut her eyes for a few seconds then opened them and faced him again. Her expression was hard with determination. "Please don't make this more difficult than it is."

He stared at her, frozen. He blinked, expecting to suddenly wake up and discover he'd been in a weird dream.

"I'm going to make it as hard as I want. I'm not letting you go without a fight." His heart seemed to know what was best, so he allowed it to guide the conversation.

He sure as hell wasn't about to let the best thing that ever happened to him walk out the door when he could do something about it. "This past week ranks among the best days of my life, Trish."

She wasn't looking at him again.

"Is this hard for you to hear?" he asked. "Would you prefer I bottled it all inside the way you're doing?"

"I'm not bottling anything inside."

"Then look at me and tell me this week hasn't been great."

She didn't turn immediately, but when she did, she regarded him with a cold hard stare that nearly immobilized his heart, and he realized for the first time he may have been completely wrong about her.

"This week *has* been great," she said. "That's not a surprise. We make magic when we touch, but great sex and a baby don't mean we should get married, which is what you've been trying to bully me into this whole time."

He swore. "Bullying you?"

Her words hit him like a cannonball, shattering any hope he'd held of convincing her they were meant to be. It was the look of indifference in her eyes, though, that undid him. It yanked him to one morning years ago when his life changed forever.

He turned away, trying to shut it out, but once he'd opened the door, the images flooded his mind unhindered. His mother stood, arms crossed and eyes as cold as ice. *I just got a gig at the Monsoon. The manager said if I'm good I could get a recording contract. Taking care of kids will just get in the way.* She hadn't known Ty and Gabby had been hiding behind the door listening.

Their aunt had spent twenty minutes trying to convince her sister her life wasn't over, that her children, not her voice, were her legacy.

Ty managed to shut out the memory once again, locking it safely at the back of his mind and made a mental note to throw away the key. He faced Patricia again.

"No, what has been happening here is me opening up to you, pouring my heart out to you, and you've made yourself judge and jury of what Ty Webber is capable or incapable of doing."

She winced, perhaps at the hardness of his tone. Or maybe hearing the truth hurt. Well, tough.

"It doesn't matter what I've been trying to show you, because you haven't been listening. While I thought we were making a go of this, you've just been biding your time, counting days. What an idiot I must have looked to you."

"Ty, come on—"

He raised his hand, cutting her off. "You know what, Patricia, save it. You win. From now on, the only thing between you and me is our child. Nothing more, nothing less."

Moisture stung his eyes. He blinked, taking in a deep breath. He needed to get out of there before he embarrassed himself by crying or worse, begging her to reconsider.

"I'm going to take a shower. When I get back, please don't be here."

He grabbed the shopping bag and forced his legs to take him to the bedroom where he shut the door and leaned against it. Taking a deep breath, he rubbed his chest, wishing he could reach in and rip his heart out. Surely that would cause him less agony.

A part of him hoped she'd suddenly realize what she was giving up and come to him. He'd fallen so hard for her, if she returned and told him she'd made a mistake, he'd take her back without a second thought. *Pathetic.* That's what he was. He'd gone against every guy code in the book and jumped in with both feet. *Look where that got you, buddy.*

He heard footsteps and perked up. The next thing he heard was the front door opening and closing, the sound setting in stone Patricia's decision.

℮ↃℇↃ

"He's not talking to me," Patricia confessed to Naaki a week later when they met for breakfast at Infusions.

They'd just finished an early morning appointment with her dressmaker to resize her maid of honor outfits for the traditional and white wedding ceremonies, since she'd filled out a little due to the pregnancy. Thankfully, she still didn't look pregnant, just curvier, and the dress-maker had even complimented her on her figure. At the compliment, guilt had jolted through her, and her heart had constricted with a stark reminder of the reason for her new curves and the man responsible for it...the man she'd lost forever.

"I don't understand. You two seemed so happy just two weeks ago," Naaki said, bringing her back to the present. Besides, didn't he talk to you at lunch yesterday?"

"Not directly to me, and nothing that wasn't wedding related." Tears misted in her eyes, but she blinked them away. "Yesterday was the first time I'd seen him since last week."

"I thought it was a little odd he didn't offer to take you home like he usually does, but Thane said I might be reading too much into things." A few seconds elapsed as they brewed their tea. "Are you finally going to tell me what happened?"

Patricia didn't respond immediately. Instead, she poked the ginger and lemon teabag, wanting a thicker brew. After a moment, she looked up. "By now, I expected you to have conscripted Thane to wheedle it out of Ty."

"You're stalling, Pat," Naaki said. "Besides, Thane tried, but Ty isn't talking either."

Patricia took in a deep breath, exhaling through her mouth. The idea of talking about Ty, reliving the break up, his words, the look in his eyes...they all made her heart twist in several painful knots. She picked up the mug, but her hands shook so much she had to set it back down. Perhaps talking would help. With a resigned sigh, she told Naaki the highlights of the break up.

"I messed up big time," she ended. "Now he won't take my calls or reply my texts unless it's wedding or baby related."

"You hurt him, Pat."

"I know." A tear fell down her cheek and she swiped it away. "The grant people called and basically told me I could only be considered if I remain single, and I wanted a moment to myself to gather my thoughts. The next thing I knew, he was asking me to leave."

"You didn't discuss it with him, Pat. You decided on your own what's best for you as if he doesn't bring anything to your life."

She sniffed, blinking back fresh tears. "I guess it's true what they say. You don't know what you have until it's gone."

"Do you love him?"

Patricia nodded. "I do." She released a breath and let the words sink in. She'd known he affected her more than any man she'd ever met. She'd known she cared about him more than she'd cared for anyone. She'd also come to accept that his return to America would devastate her. However, this was the first time she'd admitted it out loud that she loved Ty. "I love him," she repeated. "I didn't realize it until it was too late. How stupid is that?"

"You're being hard on yourself," Naaki said softly. "You haven't been in a real relationship before. Typical Pat doesn't let any man get close enough to hurt her."

"It felt great and scary," she said. "Mostly great."

Fresh tears formed. The past week, she'd cried than she had her entire life. The only time she'd felt this level of heartache had been the day it had finally sunk in that her father would never return. Even then, she'd cried a day or two before picking herself up and moving on.

"It's not too late," Naaki said. "Once he calms down a bit he'll hear you out."

Patricia shook her head. "You didn't see his face. He's not going to forgive me."

"Don't be so sure. He's already rearranged his plans for you, I'm certain he'll forgive you."

Patricia frowned. "Rearranged his plans? What are you talking about?"

"I guess he didn't get a chance to tell you. He's staying until the baby is born."

The words seeped through Patricia's consciousness sounding unreal. "What?"

She shook her head, certain now she'd slipped into a daydream where she could entertain delusions of having her desires fulfilled. Or maybe this was a reality show about to reveal exactly how badly she'd screwed up any chances of a future with Ty.

Naaki's voice jolted her back. "I'm saying he's staying."

Patricia's first instinct would have been to question it, but for the first time she didn't want to pick anything apart. Him staying meant she had time to win his love. Hope flickered to life within her.

Naaki's hand closed around hers. "If you're going to cry at my wedding, I want it to be happy tears, so it's time to start planning Operation Woo Ty." She grimaced.

"Sounds like a taekwondo move, but it's the first thing that came to mind."

Despite herself, a chuckle broke forth and hope bloomed in Patricia's heart for the first time that week.

⋘⋙

Ty's phone vibrated before it rang. He picked it up and stared at Patricia's name flashing on the screen. His thumbs lingered on the answer button for several seconds, his pulse racing, while every cell in his body begged him to press it. He longed to hear her voice. More than that, he yearned to hold her in his arms again. She, however, had made her position clear. He had no place in her heart. If only *his* heart would accept this and move on.

As he struggled with indecision, the ringing stopped. He released the breath he'd inadvertently been holding. He'd get over her. Eventually. In a few months' time, he'd have mastered the art of indifference, and their conversations would be limited to dirty diapers, doctors' appointments, and daycare fees.

"She could be calling to kiss and make up," Thane said.

Or she could be calling to tell him to stop being juvenile and get over it already so they could pick up where they left off.

"Unlikely," he replied. "Besides, we both said what needed to be said. End of story."

Ty focused his eyes on the upscale neighborhood they were driving through on their way to the airport to pick up Thane's parents. Then they had a long drive ahead of them to Kasoa, a town on the outskirts of the city where Naaki's parents lived.

With the wedding barely one week away, Naaki's

parents had invited Mr. and Mrs. Aleksander to spend the day in their home. Luckily, Ty had learned Patricia had her last client appointment before the wedding and would not be present. A fact he was immensely thankful for, since he didn't have to test his resolve or his heart by having to sit in close proximity with her and not do something stupid like forget they were done or kiss her.

He wouldn't be so lucky tomorrow, though. Plans were already in place to hold rehearsals for the customary marriage ceremony over the next two days.

He kept an unfocused stare outside, but his mind never veered too far from thoughts of Patricia. He'd successfully fielded her calls for nearly two weeks now, but he might not be so lucky the next two days. There would be family gatherings, rehearsals, dinners—all things guaranteed to make him think of home and family, and inevitably her.

God, he missed her. If this was her effect on him after only one week of living together, then he should probably be grateful she'd ended it now rather than later when her departure would have shattered him. Even so, she'd left a mark on him. He belonged to her, whether she'd have him or not.

As if on cue, the radio started playing, "You've got it bad" by Usher.

Ty muttered a curse.

"I have to admit," Thane said. "I had some doubts when you first told me you proposed, but I've never seen you like this, man."

"Yes, fool that I am, right?" The words came out through gritted teeth. He flexed his fingers, wishing he could shake some sense into her. "How can one woman be so damn stubborn?"

"I know this is a first for you, Ty, but you have to give her a chance."

"To do what exactly?" Twist the knife she'd already stuck in his chest? "She made her stance clear. She doesn't need me. We may be having a baby together, but to her I might as well be the mail man."

"I'm not hearing the part where you declared your undying love to her."

Ty snorted. "Just so she can laugh and throw it back in my face? No, thank you. I do still have some goddamn pride left."

Thane cut him a sideways glance. "Pride goeth before a fall."

Ty shot him a look, but upon seeing the teasing smile on his friend's face, he shook his head. "You don't know what you're talking about."

"Maybe I do."

He frowned. "Do you know something?"

"I shouldn't be the one telling you this."

"Come on, man. I've been wracking my brain wondering what the hell I did to drive her away, so if you know something, don't leave me hanging."

"It isn't something you did," Thane said. "She has an opportunity to win a grant she applied for, but only single women, especially single mothers, are eligible."

"What?" Ty hadn't expected her to be able to hurt him any more than she already had, but this new bit of information obliterated whatever remained of his heart. "Why didn't she tell me this?" He shook his head. "You know what, don't answer. She didn't tell me because she's bent on showing me just how little she needs me."

Still reeling, he turned away, resuming his pastime of staring outside the car window, yet he couldn't shut Patricia out of his mind. He'd seen her four times since she walked out of his door.

Each time, the sight of her alone had nearly undone him. It had surprised him just how hard he'd had to fight the urge to touch her just to have a physical connection.

The last time, just two days ago, he'd nearly given in and begged her to take him back, even on her terms—friends or co-parents with benefits—but he hadn't been able to say the words. His love for her wouldn't allow him to utter something he knew to be a lie.

He may be able to get her back in his bed with those words, but that would give him temporary relief. The instant gratification of sleeping with her would never satisfy him. Not in the long run. He needed all of her or nothing.

And from what Thane said, it looked like the odds were leaning toward nothing.

Chapter 21

Operation Woo Ty was officially a bust.

Since Patricia's chat with Naaki, she'd tried talking to Ty on occasions they'd met for wedding activities. Each time, he found some excuse not to be alone with her. She'd even gone to his place a couple of times and not found him there. Either that or he'd deliberately not answered the door. All of which said one thing.

They were over.

If she hadn't managed to get one-on-one time with him before, then chances of success were next to zero today, a week before the nuptials, stuck amid family and a flurry of wedding activities. Ironically, before now, pre-wedding activities had been her saving grace. Focusing on the various tasks helped to keep her mind off the pain in her heart and the serving of guilt it came with. A task, which proved ten times harder every time she had to be in the same room as Ty.

God knew how difficult it had been, putting on

smiles and laughs pretending she was fine when her heart lay in pieces.

Focus on the baby. She repeated those words to herself as she tried not to think about what she'd lost. Someday when Ty started talking to her again, they'd come to an arrangement regarding the baby, and she'd just have to find a way of surviving a lifetime with him being in her child's life without really being in hers.

If she managed to get through the next seven days until the wedding, that is.

"Pat?" A voice reached through her thoughts, bringing her back to the present.

Wedding rehearsals were normally reserved for the church ceremony, but for the benefit of Thane's parents they were having one for the customary wedding as well.

They'd gathered on the front porch of the house, the bride's family and friends on one side, and the groom's people on the other. Aside from Thane's parents, the groom's side constituted of a few staff who worked for Thane.

A coffee table had been set up in the middle. Next Saturday, it would be covered with a beautiful white silk table cloth. The bride was inside, waiting to be summoned, while the groom and his close friends passed time outside the walled compound, also awaiting to be escorted in at the appropriate time.

On her right sat one of Naaki's aunts, the one who'd interrupted her thoughts.

"Are you all right? You seem unusually quiet," Naaki's aunt asked.

"Yes, aunty," she answered. "I'm just tired."

The older woman smiled. "This will all be over soon, and you can rest properly."

"Shall we begin?" one of Naaki's uncles said, standing in for the head of the household.

The ceremony began with introductions from each side. They'd hired a professional wedding spokesperson to speak on behalf of the groom's family. Once the pretend gifts had been offered to the bride's family, Naaki's uncle requested for the groom to be brought in.

Patricia held her breath as someone went to call Thane and his entourage. Soon, he entered with his train of three women and three men. Her eyes immediately zoomed in on Ty. He was wearing a shirt over blue jeans that glorified his sculpted body, and she couldn't take her eyes off him.

Per the custom, they had to shake hands with members of both families. Patricia's breath hiked as she realized for the first time that sitting in the front row had been a bad idea.

With mounting excitement mixed with trepidation, she shook the three women who led the team, then Thane, and behind him, Ty. Her hungry gaze raked up his body, her mind thinking of all the times she'd had the privilege of being wrapped around him.

He proffered his hand, and as she took it, her eyes collided with his icy green gaze which held none of their usual warmth. For the two seconds he held her hand, his eyes told her she no longer held a special place in his heart.

When he released her and moved on to the next person, she tried not to break down in tears.

The rest of the ceremony progressed smoothly with Thane confirming his intentions toward Naaki, who was then brought in by members of her family. Naaki, in turn, had to indicate her acceptance of the gifts.

All the while, Ty observed the customs with rapt attention, his gaze never wavering to where she sat. She'd taken for granted the attention he'd lavished on her, and now that he'd withdrawn it, she realized she'd do anything to get it back. In fact, she already tried, but it was too little too late.

She pushed away the thoughts, as the wedding planner took center stage.

"Thank you, everyone. We'll have a fifteen-minute comfort break, then we can take it from the top a couple more times before heading back to Accra for dinner."

As she followed with a few more announcements, Patricia suddenly noticed the chairs on either side of Ty were empty. This was her chance.

Gathering up courage, she stood. As she stepped toward him, he turned as if he'd been aware of her all along.

Willing him to stay put, she took a step. Though they sat barely three meters apart, it might as well have been a mile with his hard, unreadable gaze trained on her.

She stopped in front of him. "Hi."

"Hello, Patricia."

Her heart dropped at his use of her full name, but she pushed aside her hurt, knowing she had herself to blame for it.

"Can we talk?"

For a second, something flashed in his eyes, but it was gone before she could decipher it. "Is everything okay?"

His gazed dropped to her stomach, giving implication to his question. Of its own volition, her hand moved to her abdomen, then realizing what she'd done, she pretended to smoothen her dress.

"Yes," she said.

"Then whatever you have to say can wait."

As she began to speak again, a hand closed around her arm. She turned and found the wedding planner.

"I'm sorry to interrupt, but the maid of honor is needed inside."

"Could you give me five minutes?" she said to the wedding planner.

She turned back to Ty, but to her disappointment, her gaze collided with an empty seat.

છઝઝ

Ty didn't stop walking until he'd gone past the gate. Only then did he pause in stride to consider his actions. If Thane wasn't his best friend, he'd consider quitting the wedding, because every time he thought he had a handle on his emotions, something happened to thrust him right back into her snare.

A slight breeze lessened the effect of the mid-afternoon sun. Nonetheless, he found refuge under one of three palm trees in front of the house.

He was a glutton for torture, no doubt, because from the moment he'd walked into the compound with the guys, his eyes had sought her. She'd looked so beautiful in her plain white silk shirt and chunky jewelry. His eyes had taken in the view of her shapely legs afforded by a flounced, knee-length skirt.

He cursed, remembering the softness of her palm as their hands touched in that too-brief handshake. He hadn't wanted to let go, but he'd had the presence of mind to curb his desire and force his legs to move forward.

As someone interested in the traditions of Africa, he'd hoped the rehearsal ceremony would enable him to push her out of his mind for a few minutes, but he'd been unable to concentrate, instead expending his energy on not staring at her. Even so, he'd been aware of her the entire time, so when she'd stood, he'd noticed. This time he hadn't been able to resist looking, feasting on her as she'd approached.

Looking into her eyes, he'd noted, for the first time, the fatigue in their depths, and concern had ripped through him. Had the baby kept her up at night or had she been sleeping poorly from missing him?

He gave a snort. *Laughable.*

She'd probably had a late night, getting manicures and pedicures with the ladies or whatever women did a week before the wedding.

Get a grip, man.

"Time's up," he heard someone shout.

He exhaled and psyched himself for a second dose of Patricia as he returned to the compound. He only needed to get through the next twenty-four hours. Then he'd have to figure out how to replicate his efforts, so he didn't spend the rest of his life missing what had apparently never belonged to him in the first place.

ဢၜ

They traveled in separate cars, but for Patricia the strain of shaking Ty's hand three times without being able to talk to him continued to take its toll. While she'd relished the contact those few moments they'd touched, her heart felt like it had been passed through a grinder. She'd fought to keep her tears at bay, since Naaki had forbidden her to cry anything but happy tears at the wedding.

By the time they arrived at the venue for dinner, she could no longer contain the dam behind her eyes.

"Are you okay," Naaki whispered as they exited the car and entered the building.

"Yes," she lied. "Something got into my eye."

Naaki raised her brows, but before she could comment, the wedding planner walked up to them, saying, "I need to steal the bride for five minutes."

Naaki turned to Patricia. "Are you going to be all right?"

She nodded. "I'll just pass by the washroom to get this thing out of my eye."

"We'll gather in the lounge in front of the restaurant until everyone arrives."

Nodding, Patricia hurried to the ladies' room, where she spent several minutes dabbing her eyes and masking the effect of her tears with make-up. Satisfied her emotions were back in some modicum of control, she closed her purse. With a final look at her reflection in the mirror, she took a deep breath and blew air out of her mouth, squaring her shoulders.

I can do this. She'd survived the wedding rehearsals without breaking down completely; surely, she'd survive the dinner too.

Thankfully, Naaki had limited the guest list for today to just the wedding party, close family and friends who had come from out of town to help with preparations for the wedding. Fewer people to act happy in front of. She was even more grateful her mother, who'd be arriving in a couple of days, wasn't here today to witness the mess she'd made of things.

As she made her way toward the restaurant, she found herself admiring some of the artwork gracing the walls of the swanky hotel. The lounge came into view. From the number of people, she deduced most of the wedding party had arrived. They stood in several small groups or pairs chatting as they waited to be called in. Several seats were occupied by other hotel patrons, many seemingly having meetings over drinks.

She stopped short when her gaze found Ty. He stood with Shirley, the bridesmaid, and Patricia couldn't help noticing they stood a little removed from the rest of the group. There was barely enough space for another human to squeeze between Ty's tall masculine frame and Shirley's voluptuous figure clad in a form-fitting wrap-dress.

Something dark swept through her, propelling her forward. She wasn't sure what exactly she planned to do. She only knew she couldn't stand idly by and allow Shirley to make blatant moves on her man.

Her man. If he'd have her.

They both turned just as she reached them. She squeezed between them, forcing Shirley to step back with a gasp. Ty simply raised his brows. Before her mind had a chance to talk her out of anything, she wrapped her arms around his neck, ignoring the expressions of surprise from the others.

She stretched up and kissed him.

For one glorious moment, her heart soared as her lips and body connected with Ty's. Her whole being hummed, coming alive as his scent surrounded her. The darkness hovering over her only a few seconds back fell away, letting in familiar sensations of pleasure that only Ty had ever produced in her.

The moment was short-lived, as it occurred to her he wasn't kissing her back. She pulled away, shame blazing her face. Hot tears pooled in her eyes. Was it truly over between them? Just like that?

"I'm sorry," she said, her voice quivering. "For interrupting your conversation. I'm sorry about everything."

She held her breath, willing him to say something.

After what seemed like forever, he said, "I accept your apology."

To her horror, he turned and began walking away. Alarm shot through her with every step he took. Panic set in. She couldn't let him leave. Not without saying the things in her heart.

"I love you!"

Ty stopped walking but didn't turn.

"What happened to not letting me go without a fight?" she asked, tears flowing freely down her cheeks. "You gave up in round one. What kind of fighter does that?"

A hush had fallen over the entire room, all eyes trained on her. She didn't care. It was a do-or-die moment, and she couldn't let pride or embarrassment stop her.

"Well, I'm not letting you go without a fight, Ty Webber."

He turned and stared at her for a long moment. One corner of his lips twitched. Was it a smile? Or maybe an angry tic? "Say that again," he said.

"I'm not letting you go without a fight."

He shook his head. "Before that."

Taken aback, she replied. "What kind of a fighter—"

"Before that."

A smile. Definitely, a smile.

She sucked in a breath realizing what he wanted to hear her say. "I love you."

He exhaled audibly. "Do you really?"

She nodded. "I do."

A few seconds elapsed.

"You know what, Patricia, you don't get to do this. You can't string me along for your pleasure, give me hope, and then yank the rug from under my feet because you're too scared to trust me with your heart and happiness or just because you can. I want all of you or nothing."

"All," she said. "I give you all of me. I hold nothing back."

"What about the grant?"

Her heart thudded. "You know about the grant?"

He nodded. "I'm happy for you, Patricia. I hope you get selected."

"I withdrew my application." At his raised brows, she added, "There will be others. This one's only for single women and single mothers, but I'm in love with a guy who wants to marry me, and I was hoping he'd ask again."

"What would your answer be if he asked again?"

She smiled through her tears. "Only one way to find out."

Finally, he took a step toward her. Joy flooded her. She found herself moving forward as well. When he reached her, he took a knee.

She gasped, for even though she'd hoped he'd propose again, she hadn't expected him to do it right here, right now. He took off the ring on his pinkie and held it out to her. "T, will you be my wife?"

"Yes."

Applause and whistles erupted around them as he slipped the ring onto her finger. Fresh tears flowed down her cheeks—happy tears, just as she'd promised her best friend.

With his ring in place, Ty stood and wrapped her in his arms, capturing her lips. A moan sounded from her, as she closed her eyes and kissed him back.

When they pulled apart, they were both breathless and smiling.

"I love this woman!" Ty declared to the entire room, garnering another round of applause. He embraced her and whispered in her ear. "I love you, Patricia Owusu, and I couldn't be happier you're going to be my wife and the mother of my children."

"I love you, Ty. You are, and will always be, the only man for me."

He kissed her again, sealing their new agreement: hearts entwined together forever.

THE END

About the Author

Empi Baryeh is the award-winning author of *Most Eligible Bachelor* (Book of the year: 2017 Ufere Awards). She writes sweet and sensual African, multicultural and interracial romance and women's fiction.

Her interest in writing started around the age of thirteen after she stumbled upon a YA story her sister had started and abandoned. The story fascinated her so much that, when she discovered it was unfinished, she knew she had to complete it. Somehow the rest of the story began to take shape in her mind and she's been writing ever since. She lives in Accra, Ghana, with her husband and their two children.

Her published novels include: *Most Eligible Bachelor* (2012), *Chancing Faith* (2012), *Forest Girl* (2018) and *His Inherited Princess* (2018). Baryeh is a member of Romance Writers of West Africa, an organization that is a support group for romance writers of West African origin and/or writers who write romantic fiction set in Africa.